the GIFTED

SOPHOMORES

TERRI
BLACKSTOCK

W PUBLISHING GROUP™
www.wpublishinggroup.com
A Division of Thomas Nelson, Inc.
www.ThomasNelson.com

OTHER BOOKS BY TERRI BLACKSTOCK

Cape Refuge

Covenant Child

Evidence of Mercy

Justifiable Means

Ulterior Motives

Presumption of Guilt

Never Again Goodbye

When Dreams Cross

Blind Trust

Broken Wings

Private Justice

Shadow of Doubt

Word of Honor

Trial by Fire

Seaside

Emerald Windows

For Love of Money: Sweet Delights Anthology

Seasons under Heaven, written with Beverly LaHaye

Showers in Season, written with Beverly LaHaye

Times and Seasons, written with Beverly LaHaye

The Heart Reader

The Heart Reader of Franklin High

The Gifted

Web page: www.terriblackstock.com

This book is lovingly dedicated to the Nazarene.

CHAPTER ONE

*t*hey're going to throw us off the yearbook staff. You know
that, don't you?"

Tiffany Kramer pulled the photograph out of the develop-
ing tray and hung it on the drying line. The school's makeshift
darkroom had grown hot, but they couldn't open the black-
ened window without further ruining the pictures.

"Hey, my pictures weren't as bad as yours." Josh Canfield
adjusted his glasses on his nose. A piece of white medical tape
held the corner together. It had come unwound, and Tiffany
expected his glasses to fall apart at any second.

"It's Mo's fault." She shot a look at the black linebacker,
who stood against the wall, his arms crossed.

Disgust burned in his eyes. "My fault? How do you figure
that?"

"If you'd been there on the day that all the clubs were
supposed to get their pictures made, we wouldn't have this
problem."

"Right. The day of the big game against Central High, I'm supposed to ditch the team so I can take pictures for the yearbook. Tell that to the coach."

He stepped forward and snatched the picture of the chess club off the line. "Well, there's no use waiting for this one to dry. We might as well eighty-six it. It's so blurry you can't make out a single face." He walked down the line, snatching down the one of the band, the cheerleaders, the Fellowship of Christian Athletes.

"Look at this mess." He tossed the photos into the garbage can as though they were slimy with decay. "Why didn't they get one of the seniors to take the pictures instead of you rookies? They should have known getting a sophomore who'd never held a camera in her hand and some nerd who didn't know the shutter from the lens would be a disaster."

"Hey, I resent that." Josh snatched his glasses off. "My pictures were the best ones on the church trip we took to Brazil last year, and you know it. In fact, you made me get doubles so you could have all my prints. Furthermore, you're a stinking sophomore, too, and they let *you* take pictures all the time."

"OK, so you're a great photographer on mission trips. How do you explain this disaster?"

Josh shoved his glasses back on and grabbed the pictures back out of the trash. "I think there was something wrong with the film."

"Had to be." Tiffany set her hands on her hips. "There had to be something wrong with the film."

"Face it, guys. You're just not photographer material."

"And who said we wanted to be?" Tiffany examined the other pictures on the line. If truth were told, she'd die of embarrassment before letting the yearbook editor see the mess they'd made. But she wasn't going to tell Mo that. "It wasn't my idea to spend the whole day taking pictures of a bunch of clubs. Do you have any idea how hard it is to get a shot where people aren't crossing their eyes or sticking out their tongues? *And*, by the way, I didn't think Josh's pictures of the church trip were that hot. There wasn't one of me in them."

Mo laughed. "Just because you're Miss Sophomore Class here doesn't mean you have to be the star of the youth group."

"I'm just saying that if they were all that great, they would have had some of everybody in them. He wouldn't have left anybody out."

Josh looked stricken. "I didn't mean to leave you out. But it's hard to hit a moving target, and you and your friends were avoiding me like I carried some disease."

Tiffany grunted. "Can we just get on with this? We've got to decide which of these pictures we can use and which are going to have to be redone. I have cheerleading practice in fifteen minutes."

Mo started for the door. "Just trash them all, and I'll redo them. You talk to the principal and tell him we're going to have to call another photo shoot day."

"Oh, yeah, he'll love that," Josh said. "It already took up half a day last week. He's not going to want to give us another day."

Tiffany sat down and grabbed her backpack, then jerked out a pair of tennis shoes. She never should have joined the yearbook staff. She had better things to do than sit around worrying about a bunch of blurry dorks. "Well, what do you want to do? Get all the clubs to show up on Saturday?" She pulled off her sandals. "Most of them would rather serve detention."

"He's just going to have to let us do it on a school day." Mo came back to the table and grabbed the pictures up, then dug out the ones he'd tossed into the trashcan. "There's no way around it. I'll take the pictures in there and show him what crummy shots they are. He'll have to see it."

"What if he disagrees and makes us put these in the yearbook?" Tiffany slipped her shoe on and tied it. "He might do that, you know, just to save time."

"I've got it." Josh did a little jump. Tiffany grimaced. He was always doing stuff like that. Somebody needed to tell him it made him look stupid. "If the principal does that, we can make copies and post them on the bulletin boards in the halls. There'll be such an outcry that he'll have to comply just to keep the students from rioting."

"Yeah, that'll be the day," Mo muttered. "When anybody in this school works up passion about anything—"

Tiffany's chair started to shake, and she looked over her shoulder to see if someone had sneaked up to annoy her. The water in the trays began to slosh, like something out of one of those freak movies. Tiffany came out of her chair as a picture fell off the wall and crashed. The photographs still hanging on the line

started to sway. "Earthquake!" Tiffany grabbed Mo's arm and the back of Josh's shirt as the floor began to tremble beneath them.

"Get in the doorway!" Mo cried, but before they could do so, the ceiling began to crumble. Plaster fell all around them, and a sound like the rumble of a train assaulted them. One side of the floor caved in, and they went sliding toward the opening. Tiffany screamed.

"The table!" Josh cried. "Get under the table!" But it was too late. The walls of the building began to crumble, and Tiffany heard horror-movie sounds from the other rooms—bricks falling, mortar crashing. And screams . . .

The floor gave way beneath her feet, and suddenly she was falling. She grabbed for Mo, for Josh, for anything—but it was no use. They were falling too. Debris, ceiling tiles, and bricks piled on top of them.

Tiffany groped for something to stop her fall, but finally she hit the bottom. Jagged cement and glass rained down on her.

She could see that one wall still stood, and she inched toward it. Maybe it was a way out . . . if she could just crawl across the mounds of rubble. But the earthquake rolled again, tossing the building, wreaking havoc. The window in front of Tiffany burst, and the glass came spraying into her eyes, blinding her as the world seemed to explode around her.

• • •

Josh slid down a cracked and crumbling floor into the basement, where he could hear Tiffany screaming. He hit the bottom

and scrambled to crawl away. Maybe there was a chance he could escape burial . . . just crawl into daylight. But a deafening roar knocked him back, and a steel beam came crashing down, landing on his legs with crushing force.

He shrieked, every nerve in his body electric, shooting, piercing, stabbing . . . He was going to black out . . . or throw up . . . or just lie here with no help and no relief. He fought the sensations with ragged breaths drawn through clenched teeth. Finally, he forced words from his pain-constricted throat. "Help me! Somebody help me!"

Faintly, through a veil of agony, he heard screams all around him . . . students and teachers shouting for help . . . other voices moaning, wailing . . .

God! The cry came from the very bottom of his pain. *God, help us!*

As though to mock his plea, more debris fell, piling on top of him in a rainstorm of cement and glass, papers and computers, bringing with it an agony that seemed to have no end.

• • •

Mo hit the bottom with a thud, and all went black. When he opened his eyes, he tried to orient himself, but confusion spun through his head.

He heard the sound of Tiffany's screams, Josh's agonizing yells . . .

They all lay buried in the debris of the earthquake, and he wondered why they weren't dead. He tried to shift, to look for

Tiffany and Josh, but he couldn't move. Ashes, mortar, and sawdust seemed to fill his mouth and nose, and he choked, struggling to pull in air.

Then he smelled it. Smoke.

Horror gripped him as he struggled to see where it came from. "Something's burning! Somebody help! Fire!"

"Oh, no!" Tiffany's voice quivered with terror. "We're gonna die."

"I don't smell smoke," Josh groaned. "Where is it?"

Mo looked to his right. A bright orange light glowed through the cracks of debris. The earthquake wasn't enough. Live burial wasn't the end. They were going to burn to death. He tried to move back from the fire, but something held him.

Then he saw the flames, flickering and dancing toward him, taunting, feathering through the cracks and under the rubble, licking and growing . . .

"It's over here by me!" Fire seeped into the pocket where he lay, and he felt the heat of it stinging his face. He squeezed his eyes shut and turned his face away, but the smoke was engulfing him, blanketing his face, hissing into his lungs. The earthquake had stopped, and all had fallen silent . . . except for the lethal crackle of flames next to him and the distant sound of sirens somewhere on the other side of the rubble that had been their two-story school.

The searing smoke burned his throat, scorched his lungs, blistered his vocal cords. He squeaked out his calls for help, but doubted anyone could hear. Finally Tiffany's voice reached him from across the room.

"Mo? Josh?"

"I'm here—" Josh called, "but my legs are crushed. I can't move."

"I can't see," Tiffany cried. "My eyes have glass in them, and I can't see a thing. There's something wet all over my face. I think it's blood. We've got to get out of here."

"Mo, where are you?" Josh called.

Mo tried to answer. "I'm here. Fire."

"Mo, you've got to get away from the fire somehow." Josh's voice was strained, as if he spoke through crushing pain. "Can you move?"

Mo tried to wiggle to his side, so that he wasn't facing the flames.

"Try to tunnel your way over here where there's fresher air."

Mo tried to pinpoint Josh's voice. "Where are you?" The words were barely a whisper.

"I think I'm to your left," Josh called. "I can't move my legs but I'll try to dig through with my arm."

Mo heard the sound of scraping and caught his breath as the debris next to him started to move.

"Tiffany!" It was Josh again. "Can you breathe?"

"Yes," she cried. "Mo, come on. You've got to fight your way over here."

He tried to turn his body but several heavy objects wedged him in. He was pinned here, and the fire was growing hotter, the smoke thicker. Panic drove him, and he clawed at the rocks and Sheetrock and metal and mortar. *Please God . . . Help me, Jesus . . .*

He managed to slide to his left, holding his breath against the smoke. He had to get to an air pocket before smoke inhalation killed him. It would be horrible to survive this earthquake only to be killed by smoke. He dug with his hands toward the sound of Josh's voice until finally he reached a steel beam lying across Josh's legs.

Mo felt up until he reached Josh's pants leg. Josh's hand groped down to his and grabbed it.

"I got you," Josh said. "Just try to get through here until you can breathe."

Mo snaked his way through the rubble until he finally gasped in a breath of fresher air. "I'm here." His voice was a broken squeal.

"OK, now where are you, Tiffany?" Josh's voice carried over the rubble.

"It sounds like I'm to your left, Josh." Her voice cracked. "But I don't know for sure. I can't see a thing."

Mo wondered if Tiffany's blindness or Josh's legs or his own seared lungs mattered, or if they would all see the final minutes of their lives tick away right here.

"You don't sound like you're very far away." Josh coached her with a steady voice. "Try to reach toward me, and I'll see if I can grab your hand."

There was the sound of digging, then Mo heard some broken concrete and debris shift and fall away.

"There . . . I see your hand . . ." Josh's voice quivered. "There! I've got you. We're all together. We're all OK."

"We're *not* okay," Tiffany cried. "We're buried under a two-story building, and nobody is ever going to find us!"

"Yes, they will," Josh said. "We just need to wait. We've got air, and the earthquake is over." But as the words came out, an aftershock rumbled beneath them.

Tiffany screamed. "It's starting up again!"

Mo tried to get his arm up to cover his head, and braced himself as he heard more mortar crumbling just behind him . . . then silence.

The heat behind him cooled. The smoke gave way.

"I think it put the fire out," Mo squeaked out.

"Well, that's something now," Josh said. "Isn't that something? We can't give up. We've got to keep holding hands. Let's not let each other go. We'll get through this together. We know what to do."

"What?" Tiffany cried.

"We can pray." Josh's hand trembled as Mo clutched it. "All the stuff we've learned in youth group, we can use it now. It's like all those lessons Jerry's done for us lately on suffering and crises. Maybe all that was God's way of preparing us for this. We've just got to believe and trust and ask God to help us."

Mo wished he felt Josh's confidence, but the fear was too strong. Here he was, the big athlete, and Josh was just the little nerd that everyone ignored. Yet Josh was the one holding them together.

"Will you lead us first, Josh?" Tiffany asked. "And then I'll go next."

"OK. And then Mo, you can pray silently. Your voice is pretty much shot, so you don't need to be using it."

Mo didn't argue with that.

He lay still, terrified, his heart racing and palms sweating, bleeding and in pain. Josh began to pray. "Dear Lord, You know where we are. We're not hidden from You."

The prayer calmed Mo, focused his thoughts, gave him more peace than he'd felt since the very first tremor. Maybe it would be all right. Maybe the Lord would choose to save them.

*e*very breath was agony, but Mo kept holding Josh's hand as if it were his only link to life. He listened as Josh and Tiffany took turns praying—deep, heartfelt, wrenching prayers that God would keep them from being buried further, that He would continue to supply them with the air that kept them alive, that someone would hear their cries and dig deep enough and fast enough to pull them from the rubble before it was too late.

And they prayed for the others who'd been in the building, engaged in various after-school activities. They bargained and pleaded and made promises to be better warriors for God's kingdom.

But no one came.

Seconds slithered into minutes; minutes crawled into hours.

"So this is what it's like to die." Tiffany had stopped crying, and her voice sounded as if she'd given up. "My mom . . ." She groaned again, and the mournful sound broke Mo's heart. "I can't even imagine what she's going to feel." Her voice broke, and he heard her muffled sobs. "My parents couldn't have any more children after me. What are they going to do?"

"Hush," Josh said. "You're not going to die."

"My dad will mourn for years." The statement came in a quiet monotone. "They'll probably divorce over it. That's what happens, you know. When a couple loses a child, the marriage has too much strain and they sometimes wind up divorced."

"Tiffany, we have to believe God is going to answer our prayers."

Mo wanted to agree with Josh, but he couldn't get his scorched vocal chords to work.

Tiffany wasn't satisfied. "But hasn't Jerry taught us that sometimes God answers no? Sometimes He has other plans?"

Mo closed his eyes. Why couldn't Tiffany just shut up? He couldn't think about God answering no. If he could speak, he would tell them that they couldn't give up. The moment they gave up, it would be the end of them. He tried to relax his head back, drawing air in, grimacing at the pain in his tortured throat. How long had it been since the quake? The best he could figure, it had been three hours, maybe four. It was pitch-black where they lay, and the dust and rubble choked Mo as he lay in the silence. He still clutched Josh's clammy hand, but his arm was going numb. He needed to move it, but he didn't dare break that contact. He needed to know that Josh was still there . . . moving . . . clinging . . . keeping them together.

He felt his own panic rising up to his throat. He should never have wished for Tiffany to shut up. No, he didn't want silence, after all. He needed to hear their voices, reminding him that he wasn't alone. But he wasn't able to say so.

He could hear Josh's breathing, Tiffany's sniffing. Debris creaked around him, and he listened for every sound, every movement, fearing that the fire would spring back to life or that more mortar and wood would shift. Sweat trickled into his eyes, and he wished he could raise his arm and brush it away.

Finally he heard Tiffany's voice again. "Josh? Mo? I'm really sorry for the way I've treated you guys."

Mo hadn't expected that from her, and he frowned, waiting to hear more. Josh spoke for him. "You haven't treated us badly."

Mo almost choked. Tiffany treated Josh as if he was scum on her shoe.

"Well, I haven't been all that nice, either," Tiffany said. "I mean, we're brothers and sisters in Christ, and half the time I treat you like you're beneath me or something. I'm such a jerk."

"You're not a jerk," Josh said. "If I were a popular cheerleader, I'd probably treat the class nerd the same way."

"You're not the class nerd."

Boy, they were really shoveling the lies around now. Mo couldn't believe it.

But Tiffany wasn't finished. You would have thought that Josh was the only one who could pull her out of this mess, and she had to butter him up so he'd do it. "You're really smart, and you're good in a crisis. I mean, look at you now. You're the one who got us holding hands and calmed us down. You may have even saved Mo's life by getting him to come this way."

Shame crept over Mo, and he closed his eyes. Tiffany was right. Josh *had* saved his life.

Her voice lowered a degree. "Next time we're on a mission trip, I promise not to avoid your camera and then complain about you not having any pictures of me."

Josh's grip loosened on Mo's hand. "Well, while we're confessing, I guess I ought to tell you I'm sorry for calling you a snob."

"You called me a snob?"

Mo couldn't help smiling at the confession.

"Yeah," Josh said, "but only to a few of the kids at church, and I'm sorry they agreed with me. I'll never do it again."

It was Tiffany's turn to be quiet. She was miffed, Mo thought. Probably mentally calling Josh names again.

But Tiffany surprised him. "It's OK. It's probably true. I am a snob. And, Mo? Can you hear me?"

Mo squeezed Josh's hand.

"He's listening," Josh said.

"I'm sorry I'm such a racist," Tiffany said. "I mean, I tolerate you and everything because you're a starting linebacker and I'm a cheerleader, but I haven't really wanted to be friends with you because . . . well, you're not like me. But you're my brother in Christ . . . and now it looks like we're brother and sister in crisis, too."

Brother and sister in crisis. Mo liked that. The truth was, he couldn't blame her for her attitude toward him, when he'd had his own bias against her. Mo squeezed Josh's hand again. "He said it's OK," Josh said.

"He did?" Tiffany asked. "Are you sure?"

"Yeah," Josh said. "He says he can't hold it against you because he calls you a white preppy all the time, which, if you think about it, is just as racist as what you've thought of him."

Mo punched at Josh's hand. He hadn't said anything of the sort! Then he relaxed. He might not have said it, but he had thought it. Josh really had his number.

"I forgive you, Mo," Tiffany said, "if you'll forgive me."

Mo squeezed Josh's hand twice, for emphasis.

Josh seemed to understand. "Mo says it's a deal."

For the first time since they'd been trapped Tiffany was able to laugh. "Are you sure he's saying all these things, Josh?"

"Yeah." Josh laughed too. "And if you don't believe me, you can confirm it when we get out of here."

Silence fell over them again.

"Do you think we'll really get out of here?" Tiffany's question cut through the quiet. "Or are our faces just going to be on the tube for the next month as people cry and mourn over us and talk about what great kids we were?"

Mo closed his eyes, but couldn't escape the image of his family standing over his grave.

Josh didn't answer right away. "Why do they always lie about you when you're dead? Why can't they just tell the truth? 'He was the biggest jerk I knew, and nobody liked him.' It would be more helpful to people to say that than to paint him out to be some person that nobody even recognizes."

Tiffany sniffed, and Mo knew she was starting to cry again.

"I know if I did die I'd go to heaven and everything, but I haven't done that much in my life. I've been pretty worthless. There's so much I should have been doing."

"What should you have been doing, Tiffany?" Josh asked.

"I don't know. Helping people. Loving them the way Christ said to do. That was the main thing, you know. To love people. He said they would know we were Christians by our love. Only I haven't done that very well."

Mo shook his head. He hadn't done that well, either.

Would they really die here, like this? He'd known a couple of kids who'd died in tragic car accidents. It seemed as though they always left behind a diary or something, talking about death . . . like they knew ahead of time it was coming. They'd tell someone that they thought they were going to die young, in an airplane crash or of some disease. They'd write songs about death and heaven and leave them for people to find.

He hadn't written any songs.

The truth was, half the people in the school didn't even know he was a Christian. He'd been too busy blending in and making himself look good to think about sharing his faith. Now, if he survived this quake, he wondered if he'd ever be able to use his voice again. He should have told people while he could. He should have been shouting about Christ's love from the mountaintops. But he'd been too worried about what people would think of him.

If Jerry, the youth minister, preached at his funeral and talked about Mo's Christianity, what would they think? Mo shook his head. He could just see his school friends now, scratching their heads, wondering if Jerry was talking about the same Mo they all knew.

"My eyes are caked shut," Tiffany went on. "I can't see a thing. But it's almost like I deserve it. I walked around with my nose in the air and never saw anybody. I'd pass you guys in the hall and never even look at you. I wish I had seen with God's eyes."

Josh cleared his throat, shaking Mo from his dismal thoughts. Pain thinned Josh's voice. "Well, this seems so stupid now . . . but I have to admit that I've been a little focused on my grades. I know Mo's competitive in athletics and all, but if I'm not number one in the class, I punish myself for days. My mind hasn't exactly been on doing unto others. I sit in my bedroom, studying and studying, never asking God where He'd really like me to go. And now I may not be going anywhere. I may never be able to use my legs again."

Tiffany's voice held a note of defeat. "Do you think if we die that they'll say we were self-centered, fruitless, and lukewarm? I mean after the funeral, when people are getting real on the phone and stuff, when they're being honest."

"No." There was no doubt in Josh's voice. "People are superstitious about speaking ill of the dead. But Jerry will preach each of our funerals, all sad and miserable about losing us, and he'll make people think we were really great." His voice rose slightly in pitch. "I wonder how many more he's losing today."

Mo shook his head. *Please, God, no others.* With any luck,

there weren't many kids at school . . . most of the cheerleaders had probably been outside, and the football players might have already dressed out and gone to the field. He tried to think of the other after-school activities that would have kept students in the building. "It's not just our school, either," Tiffany said. "There are probably people buried all over town, like us. It could take days for them to even work their way to the school to start digging us out. How long can you live without food and water?"

"A long time." The words seemed to knock the breath out of Josh. "Maybe we just need to concentrate on the Bread of Life and the Living Water. He's the only one who can keep us alive now anyway."

With that, Tiffany finally fell silent. Mo was glad, for she seemed to voice the most desperate of his thoughts—things that left terrifying images lingering in his brain—when what he needed to concentrate on were the tiny filaments of hope unwinding at the back of his mind.

CHAPTER THREE

*t*he weight of the rubble pressing down on Mo reminded him of an Alfred Hitchcock flick he'd seen once—or was it a *Twilight Zone* episode?—where the ceiling and floor moved closer together, mashing the frantic actor as he scrambled to find an escape. Mo couldn't remember if the room was some kind of torture chamber or what, or even how it had ended. But sweat beaded in his hair and prickled his armpits, and though concrete, mortar, and wood pinned him in place, he saw himself as that actor, fighting to hold the ceiling up with his hands and the floor back with his head and feet before they crushed the life out of him.

Then he heard the sound . . . a scraping over their heads . . . distant voices . . .

"Did you hear that?" Josh shook Mo's hand, as if to wake him from despair. "I heard something!"

Mo listened again, ears straining, aching to hear, his mind taking him up through the rubble toward the sounds they'd heard.

"We have to make noise!"

Tiffany proceeded to do just that. "Help! Please help us! We're buried here. Please help us!"

Josh joined in, yelling at the top of his lungs.

Mo tried to make a sound, too, but his voice sounded like ripping paper. Helpless, Mo prayed instead. *Lord, let them hear us. Please help them get to us.*

The sound of power tools silenced them . . . and they seemed to hold a collective breath. Josh's grip on Mo's hand was stronger now, and he clung back. He knew that Josh had Tiffany's hand too. He had never been more thankful for someone's touch.

The rubble burying them groaned and moved; debris crumbled and shifted.

"What if the movement makes things worse?" Tiffany asked.

"Just don't let go of my hand," Josh said and started to yell again. Tiffany joined in, and the two of them yelled and screamed until their voices were hoarse.

Finally an answer came. "How many of you are down there?"

Laughter started in the deepest part of Mo's belly, working its way up to his throat and whistling out of him. They would be rescued! He would not be crushed to death. There was hope, after all.

"Three, that we know of," Josh called up. "We're all injured."

"Hold tight. We're coming."

Power tools buzzed more loudly now, and finally Mo heard the sounds of shovels digging, men yelling, sirens blaring.

He'd heard accounts before of near-death experiences, where

the injured had seen a white light at the end of a dark tunnel and it beckoned them toward it. When light broke through the darkness of the destruction around Mo, he started laughing again. He felt the cool, fresh air sweeping away the thick, dusty, death-threatening air, and he sucked in a breath.

Unfortunately, his lungs couldn't handle it, and he started to cough, each contraction scraping the blistered tissue of his lungs and throat.

He saw the silhouettes of people digging, watched the hole growing bigger, felt the weight of debris being lifted from them.

They found Tiffany first. "My eyes," she said in that shaky voice. "I can't see."

"We're getting you out," a voice said. "Just hang on."

"No, I'm all right," she said. "The others are probably worse. Mo breathed in smoke . . . and Josh's legs . . ."

Shouting ensued, and Mo saw rescuers working their way toward them, trying to figure out the best way to get them out. Firefighters with tools and shovels picked the debris away, piece by piece, clearly careful not to make things worse.

They pulled Tiffany out first, strapped her onto a gurney, then slid her through the fragile tunnel they had created for her rescue. "Oh, no, look at her eyes," Mo heard someone say.

"Can't get the blood off of her face with all the glass . . ."

". . . needs immediate attention if she's ever going to see again . . ."

"Call my mom, please!" Tiffany's voice rose above the melee. "Please, somebody call my mom."

The power tools started working again, and Mo figured they were coming for him. "We've got to get Josh before we can reach you," someone shouted to Mo. "Are you OK? Anything we need to know?"

Mo squeezed Josh's hand, and Josh said, "He's OK. He just can't talk. There was a fire at the beginning, and he breathed in a lot of the smoke."

"Is he conscious?"

"Yes. I've got his hand, and he's squeezing it. I think he wants you to hurry."

Mo knew Josh spoke for himself, but it was OK with him if they hurried. He watched as they lifted the beam that had crushed Josh's legs. Josh cried out, but didn't let go of Mo's hand. Mo squeezed harder.

It took several moments for them to get Josh onto the gurney. All the while, Mo clung to his hand. He knew he was going to have to let go, that Josh needed medical help and couldn't hang around once he was free, but Mo couldn't seem to make his fingers release him.

Finally they pulled Josh away, and their hands separated.

Mo started to cry then—stupid, helpless tears, like a little kid waking up in a home full of strangers. He knew the rescue workers were digging for him next, that they hadn't left him alone, yet he had the sensation of lying on a mountain in the path of an avalanche. Would they get to him in time? Or would he be crushed just before they worked him free?

Then they had him, dragging him through the tunnel like

some kind of birth canal, and as he came into sunlight he felt the shock of that rebirth into a world where chaos reigned in a blur around him.

CHAPTER FOUR

*t*he cool breeze hit Tiffany's face with life-giving hope. If only she could see! She wondered if it was still daylight, or if darkness had fallen over the town. She had no idea how long they'd been there. Pain stabbed through her eyes, and above her she heard the paramedics barking out things she didn't understand about her injury. She felt herself being loaded into an ambulance, heard the siren starting up, felt the van pulling out. She wanted to see if Mo and Josh were all right, or if any of her friends were still buried or dead.

Most of all, though, she wanted her parents. What if they'd been hurt? What if they were trapped under some other crumbled building?

The ambulance reached the hospital in moments, and the doors flew open. Tiffany's gurney was jerked out, and she felt herself rolling like an actor in some bad dream. The hospital sounded like a triage unit in a rerun of *MASH*. She heard screaming and crying around her, and doctors and nurses yelling across the patients.

"Glass in the eyes—" A voice above her yelled over the jumble of voices—"Vitals are stable. She was just pulled from the rubble of Valley High."

Fingers touched her face, probed near her eyes. She cried out as someone pried her eyelids apart. Her eyes opened, but all she saw was darkness.

"I can't see! I can't see anything."

She heard another siren and voices screaming again . . . then she felt the whisk of air as whoever had been standing near her abandoned her.

"Hello? Please. Is anybody there?" She tried to feel around her, but there was no one near her gurney. They had left her alone! "Please help me. I can't see!"

She wished she could reach out and hold Josh's or Mo's hand. They had kept her from falling apart . . . from giving in to terror.

"We'll be right with you," someone yelled, "but we have to help the more critical patients first. You're OK, though. You're going to be taken care of."

"I need to call my parents." She realized she sounded like a little child. "They need to know that I'm alive." But no one listened. Tiffany tried to sit up, tried to force her eyes to see, but the mere movement of her swollen, lacerated eyelids sent pain lashing through her. Still nothing came into focus. Not even light. She dropped back down.

She was blind, and no one was doing anything to help her. She longed for her mother's face, to see her standing over her, reassuring her that everything was fine. She wished she could look into her father's eyes and see the strength there.

But she might never see again. How would she get along as a blind person? Didn't God know that she didn't have the strength of character to adapt to this kind of change in her life? Didn't He realize what was happening?

As if in answer, a thought came to her mind that God not only knew, but that He was still in control.

Her heart cried out, *Then why are You letting this go on?*

She wasn't the first to feel the terror of sudden blindness. Her mind strayed to Paul in the Bible. He'd been struck with blindness on the road to Damascus. He had been blind for three days until God sent someone to heal him. Meanwhile, God had gotten his attention.

Was He trying to get her attention too? Had it taken this to wake her out of her apathetic stupor?

"Lord, let my blindness be temporary," she whispered. "Heal me, and I promise to use my sight for Your glory."

But even as she prayed, she feared that the Lord had different plans. Maybe she truly did deserve blindness after looking right through those in her path every day. Maybe she deserved to have no sight, when she'd refused to see . . . "One more chance, Lord. Please . . . just one more chance."

• • •

Josh Canfield had passed three kidney stones in his life, but he'd never felt agony close to that in his legs now. The paramedics had loaded him into the rescue unit, and he could tell how careful they were being, but every bump and swerve in the road had sent him arching back and biting against the pain. The ambulance finally stopped, the doors flew open, and a hospital orderly helped the paramedics pull him out of the vehicle.

"Crushed legs." The paramedic handed the IV bag to the orderly. "But his vital signs are stable. He was pinned under a steel beam and buried under two floors of rubble at the high school."

Josh looked around and saw bloody patients all around him. Some he recognized as kids from his school. Others were older—business people, moms and dads, grandparents. Some looked as if they only had superficial injuries. Others lay with twisted faces, clearly in terrible pain.

Josh tried to sit up, but the pain was so great that he had to stay on his back. He looked around, trying to find Mo and Tiffany, and finally spotted Tiffany across several gurneys. Her hands flailed in the air, reaching around as if trying to catch hold of someone. Her face was covered with dried blood from the glass cuts on her skin, and her eyes had swollen almost shut and crusted over with more blood.

He choked back a sob, and pressed his fist to his mouth.

At least she was alive. But where was Mo? Had they gotten him out?

If only he had a cell phone with him so he could call his parents and tell them that he was OK, but he wasn't sure he was. The pain racked his body, and sweat dripped down his face and plastered his shirt to his skin. But he reminded himself that pain might be a good sign. Maybe there was no paralysis. Maybe he wouldn't lose his legs after all.

He tried to grab a thought lingering on the tip of his brain, a thought about someone in the Bible who'd had his hip thrown out. Whoever it was had wrestled with God and ended up with a limp for the rest of his life to show for it. Who was that? Oh, yes. Jacob. The father of the twelve tribes. Israel himself. God had wrestled him into obedience with one touch to his hip joint. Was God trying to get Josh's obedience? Would Josh even be able to limp, or would he be in a wheelchair for the rest of his life? Did people recover from injuries like this one?

"Oh, Lord, please," he whispered, "fix my legs. If You do, I'll go wherever You want them to take me." He looked over at Tiffany again. "And Lord, please help Tiffany see."

He heard another ambulance flying toward them, and he wiped the sweat from his face and squinted to see Mo being pulled out. He was on oxygen, and when the paramedics yelled something, a couple of doctors abandoned what they were doing and rushed to his side.

"And Mo, Lord. Please help Mo."

• • •

Mo woke up inside the hospital, in some kind of examination room and realized he must have passed out after they got him into the ambulance. He wanted to tell someone to call his parents, to let them know he was all right. He wanted to check on whether or not Tiffany and Josh had made it to the hospital.

Had the football team been out on the field doing warm-ups during the quake, or were most of them in the locker room? Had they been buried too? Fat tears rolled down his cheeks, and he thought of screaming out in a desperate attempt to make contact with other people he cared about. But his throat hurt so bad he couldn't even catch a breath. And he sure couldn't ask the questions on his mind.

He was as bad off as that Zacharias guy, struck dumb until his son, John the Baptist, was born. Mo tried to swallow and grimaced at the pain that ripped through his throat. Could God possibly be behind this? Maybe it was punishment for some of the stupid things he said. He'd been called insensitive, sarcastic, irreverent. Maybe he did deserve it.

But Zacharias had spoken again.

Didn't that mean there was hope for Mo? If he only had his voice back again . . . he wouldn't be so sarcastic, and he wouldn't say things that made people feel bad. He'd tell them the things that mattered. He'd tell them about Jesus.

Oh Lord . . . give me back my voice, and I'll never misuse it again.

CHAPTER FIVE

*t*iffany's parents found her a short time later and wept as if she'd died and been reborn. She buried her ravaged face against her mother's neck.

"Mom, I'm blind, and my eyes feel like ice picks are sticking in them." She turned her face up to her father. If only she could see him. "Daddy, make them do something."

"They're going to, sweetheart." His voice sounded hollow and stopped up. She pictured him waiting those five hours for word about his child. "We're trying to get you into a room right now, honey."

"But what can they do? How will they get all the glass out?"

"They're going to do some surgery, honey. Just sit tight. There's a shortage of doctors, and a lot of people who need help."

Tears dropped onto Tiffany's hands as her mother held her. "You're going to be OK, darling. You're going to be fine. I'm just so glad you're alive."

"Was anybody killed?"

The moment of silence that followed Tiffany's question spoke volumes. "Honey, we don't have a count, yet but there are a lot of people still buried."

"In the school?"

"They're not sure. No one seems to know for sure how many were there after school."

"Oh, Daddy, they've got to get them out. They've *got* to. They're probably down there holding hands and praying like we were."

"We?" her mother asked.

"Josh Canfield and Mo Frazier. You know, from church. We prayed, and God saved us. But I don't know what He's doing with my eyes."

A small commotion arose as someone entered the room—a doctor and a nurse, her parents told her—and Tiffany winced as a needle pricked into her vein. After a few moments she began to relax and drifted off into a merciful sleep.

• • •

Josh's parents had run from hospital to hospital trying to find their son. When they'd finally located him at Valley General, they rushed to his side. Josh's father, a Silicon Valley computer genius, wasn't content to let his son lie in agony while the doctors worked saving lives.

"My son is in pain!" He grabbed a passing orderly. "Help my son!"

"Sir, I can't help him. He needs a doctor. They'll be with him shortly." The man dashed off.

"Somebody come help my son!" he bellowed out. "Now, or I'll slap you with a lawsuit that'll put every one of you out of a job!"

Finally, a weary-looking nurse with blood on her scrubs stopped beside Josh's gurney. "I need to put an IV in your hand. What's your name, son?"

"Josh Canfield."

She tightened a large rubber band around his arm, tapped his veins, and quickly slid the needle in, then released the band.

He looked at the IV pole she strung up next to him. "What's that going to do?"

"It'll help you with your pain, and then we've got to get you into X-ray. The problem is, we have so many people ahead of you who are in critical condition, they'll die if they don't get priority treatment."

"Painkiller? He's going to need *surgery.*" You would have thought his father was the one with mangled legs. "He needs attention now." The nurse started away. "Hey! You'll hear from my lawyer if—"

"Tell him to talk to me," the nurse shouted back. "Be my guest."

His father swung around, more frantic than Josh had ever seen him, and looked down at Josh.

His mother, who had hung back while his father threw his fit, touched Josh's chest and leaned over him. "They're doing the best they can, Josh. Do you think you can hold on?"

What choice did he have? He really had no right to complain. At least he wasn't under that pile of rubble any longer. He shivered at the memory of how dark and desperate that had been.

People all around him moaned and cried, and death lured many of them.

And the pain was a good sign . . . it had to be a good sign.

"I'll be OK." He closed his eyes and hoped the painkiller would kick in soon.

• • •

Because Mo hadn't been able to give the doctors his name, his parents had almost given him up for one of the lost beneath the rubble. Finally another set of parents who had seen Mo pulled out had called and let them know where their son was being treated. They had rushed to his side, horrified and crying, gushing out a million questions about his condition.

Though he couldn't answer them, relief washed over him like a warm shower. They were here, and now he knew there was someone who would be his voice.

His mother wept over him, searching the faces of the doctors for someone who would help him, and his father kept his hand braced on his shoulder . . . the most blatant display of affection he'd ever gotten from the man. His father believed that hard work and providing well for his family was the way to show them he loved them.

But that hand on his shoulder told Mo so much more today. Mo's eyes grew heavy as the drugs they'd given him worked through his bloodstream. He felt himself drifting out of consciousness, into the sweet grace of sleep.

"That's my boy," his mother whispered as she stroked his forehead. "You sleep now. We'll be here watching over you."

And so he did, rising and falling in a stupor of numbness, until a restless sleep filled with dreams of rescue and air took him over.

CHAPTER SIX

*m*orning light slanted through the blinds of the hospital room window, warming Tiffany's face. Slowly, she opened her eyes.

The blinds came into focus, and she blinked at the stark, uncensored light.

"I can see!" She sat up and touched her eyes. Her lids felt soft, clean, completely unharmed. "I can really see!"

"Shhh." She turned at the sound and saw that she was not alone. Three other beds were crammed into the small room, and people in sleeping bags cluttered the floor. She looked down and saw her mother lying on a bag next to her gurney.

"Mom?" She leaned toward her mother. "Mom, wake up."

Her mother stirred, then quickly sat up. "Honey, it's all right." She got to her feet. "Are you in pai—?" She caught her breath as she saw Tiffany's eyes.

"Mom, I can see." She touched her mother's face, her hair. "You're so beautiful! I can *see* you!"

"You can?"

"Yes. My eyes . . . they don't feel cut or anything. I need a mirror."

Her mother only stared at her. "Look at you. You don't have a scratch . . ."

Tiffany's heart pounded. "A mirror, Mom."

Her mother dug through her purse and pulled out a compact. Tiffany opened it and peered at her eyes. They seemed untouched. The whites were whiter than they'd ever been, the lashes looked clean and soft, and the lids were unmarred.

Her mother slowly took her face in her hands. "Tiffany, what's happened to you?"

Tiffany stared at her reflection. Something weird had happened. "Mom, did they do surgery while I was asleep?"

"No! I hardly slept at all last night, I was so worried about how long they were waiting."

She gaped at her mother. "Are you sure?"

"They didn't do anything. They didn't even get the glass out."

"But how can I see? My vision is even better than before."

Her mother ran her fingertips across Tiffany's skin. "Look at you. Your face isn't even cut. There's not a bruise . . ." Her mother shook her head and whispered, "Tiffany, this is a miracle."

Tiffany caught her breath. They had been rescued. That was enough of a miracle. She hadn't expected another one. She slid off of the gurney and looked out the window. From a distance she could see the mountains on the horizon, something she hadn't been able to see before without wearing her glasses, which she kept tucked into her purse most of the time. But now she saw clearly.

She turned back to her mother, searching her face for an explanation. "Mom, I think I've been healed."

"You *have* been healed." Her mother started to cry. "Oh, honey, you've been healed. A real live miracle healing. Let's go tell the doctors."

• • •

"I thought you said his legs were crushed."

Josh woke at the sound of the doctor's voice. The man stood over his bed flipping through his chart. "There's nothing wrong with his legs."

"Oh, yes, there most certainly is. They were crushed by a steel beam when his school collapsed." His father still wore his tie from last night, though his shirt was wrinkled from a night on the floor. "Look at him. You can just look at him and tell—" His father's words fell off as he looked down at Josh's legs. His expression changed.

Frightened, Josh touched his leg with his hand. His skin felt normal, smooth, not like it had felt last night, with the bones bent and broken inside. And there was no pain. His legs felt normal, unharmed.

Man, those drugs really did the trick. He lifted himself up and looked down at his legs. His pants legs had been cut off, and beneath the gown someone had put on him, he could see that his legs lay normal and perfect.

"Wait!" He looked up at his father, then at the doctor. "Yesterday my legs were a mess. They were all mangled up. Crushed! How—?"

His father pulled the sheet completely off of him, his face betraying his astonishment. "There's not a scratch. Not a single bump!"

The doctor looked at his watch. "Josh, can you move your legs?"

Josh lifted his knee. His leg moved easily and without pain. The doctor set the chart down and began palpating Josh's thigh.

"There's nothing wrong with this boy's legs. Josh, tell me if you feel any pain."

Josh sat all the way up now. "No . . . they actually feel fine. I feel like I could run a marathon!"

His father loosened his tie. "You can't tell me there's nothing wrong. My son was buried under a school! They had to dig him out."

"Sir, I can send him for x-rays if it will satisfy you."

"Darn right it'll satisfy me. Last night I counted at least five breaks that I could see, and one of the doctors said that his right femur was crushed."

"But I don't feel any broken bones. I'm not in any pain," Josh said excitedly.

While his father and the doctor went back and forth, Josh slipped his legs off the side of the bed. He didn't feel any pain, so he slid down until he was standing on his feet.

His father's rambling stopped, and the doctor gestured toward Josh's legs.

"See? He's standing. If he had broken bones, I assure you he would not be standing."

"Josh?" His father gaped at him, as if Josh owed him an explanation.

"Dad, I'm fine." Josh bent his knees and bounced up and down. He threw his head back and laughed. "Look at me! There's nothing wrong with me."

"Josh, there's something strange about this."

"I've been healed." The words came out as the awareness took hold. He *had* been healed. Last night he had wondered if he'd ever walk again. He'd fallen asleep in a fog of painkiller that hadn't seemed to even touch the pain.

And now he could walk.

He'd never seen such a look on his father's face. The man stood with his mouth hanging open, scratching his tousled hair. "But they didn't do anything to you. You were waiting in line for surgery."

"But Dad, I don't *need* surgery." He jumped and did a sprint across the room, then ran back to his gurney. "Look, I'm healed. God healed me. Isn't that amazing?"

His father, who wasn't much of a believer, just gaped at him. The doctor shrugged, as if Josh had been nothing more than a misdiagnosed statistic, and left the room. But Josh knew the truth. He'd been healed. His legs felt stronger and more limber than they'd ever felt in his life. He felt as if he could do anything, go anywhere.

In fact, the sooner the better.

"Dad, I want to get out of here. What do we have to do to check me out?"

His father still gaped down at his legs. "I don't know, Josh. I'll . . . I'll look into it."

. . .

Mo woke up to the sound of humming from the machine next to his hospital bed. He was in a ward of some kind, lined up with other patients who struggled for life after the earthquake. He pulled the oxygen mask off of his face and sat up. He needed to swallow, so he steeled himself against the inevitable pain.

But there was none.

He swallowed again, easily, comfortably. His throat didn't hurt anymore! He felt as if he could breathe normally. The blisters in his mouth seemed to have cleared up. Man, they were good here! They hadn't even done that much, and already he was well. He cleared his throat, testing, and tried to speak.

"Mama?"

His mother popped up from the couch next to his bed. "Mo? You OK?" She stared up at him. "Mo . . . you spoke."

"Yeah. What did they do to me?"

"Nothing. We've been waiting for them to get to you. How is it you're talking?"

"I don't know, but I don't feel bad anymore." He rubbed his throat . . . had he dreamed the whole thing? "Mama, was there an earthquake?"

"Yes, and you were buried and had smoke inhalation!" She

got up and came to gaze into his mouth. "Mo, your throat looks normal."

He pulled the mask all the way over his head and dropped it on the bed. "Lungs feel fine, throat feels fine." He reached for the glass of water on the bed table and drank it down. It tasted better than any water he'd ever had.

He set the glass down and got out of the bed. "God is awesome. Mama, do you realize what's happened? I'm healed!"

She clapped her hands together and laughed. Mo howled out his own laughter, then started to sing "Awesome God" at the top of his perfect lungs.

A chorus of shushes sounded from around the room, and nurses rushed in. "Please, keep your voice down. Others are resting."

"But I can talk!" Mo grabbed her to dance with him.

She pulled free, then went to his chart and quickly scanned it. Her expression changed, and she took his chin and made him open his mouth. "Say 'ah'."

"Ahhhh," he said.

The nurse looked back at his chart. "Amazing."

His mother grabbed the nurse and almost danced with her herself. "Oh, something's happened, something miraculous. I believe God's answered our prayers in a way we didn't even expect. You've been healed, Mo! We've got to tell your father! They would only let one of us stay last night, so he went home."

Mo shouted out a whoop, and got shushed again. He grabbed his mother's hand. "Let's go, Mama. I'm ready to get out of this joint."

CHAPTER SEVEN

*t*iffany wove her way through the gurneys and the hospital corridor, intent on getting out of this place. Wall-to-wall people, all victims of the earthquake, waited for medical attention. She spotted her school's head cheerleader, Amanda Lewis, sitting up on a gurney a little ahead of her.

"Amanda! Amanda, are you okay?"

The girl had a bandage around her head, and blood had seeped through it. She looked disheveled and dazed, and dark circles hung under her eyes. "Yeah. I just had a concussion when something hit me in the head." She squinted at Tiffany. "I heard you were almost dead."

The words stopped her. By all rights, maybe she should have been. Tiffany looked back at her mother, who had caught up to her. "I was buried, all right, and I thought I was blind. But this morning I woke up and I was better than ever. It's really weird."

Amanda seemed unimpressed. "My mother is trying to get

them to let me go. I'm sick of being here. I didn't sleep a wink last night, and I've got a bad headache. I hate this stupid, dirt-baggy place."

Tiffany frowned. That was all Amanda could think of to say? *Didn't she hear what I said? That I was healed? Talk about self-absorbed!*

But just as Tiffany was ready to walk away, she met Amanda's eyes.

Flash.

She saw a younger Amanda—maybe six years old—hunkered in a corner of a dark room.

A man ranted as he trudged through the room. "Come out of here, you little rat. I'll find you, and when I do—" He turned the corner and found the little girl, grabbed her hand and jerked her up. His fist came down across her face, and she started to scream. The tendons under her arm snapped as he pulled her to her feet, then hit her again and knocked her to the floor. The child kept screaming.

Flash.

Tiffany closed her eyes, shook her head, then opened them again. Amanda was there, still sitting on that gurney, clutching her bandaged head. Tiffany frowned. What had just happened? She'd just been standing here looking at her friend. Was she hallucinating? Were the drugs they'd given her hanging on?

"You OK?" Amanda asked.

Tiffany stared at the girl. Had she just seen the truth of

Amanda's past? She tried to shake herself out of her thoughts. "Yeah, uh, just a little confused. Uh, maybe I have a concussion, too."

Her mother gasped. "Oh, no. Tiffany, is your vision blurring?"

"No, mom. It's real clear."

Tiffany started to walk away, and her mother followed on her heels. "Honey, what's wrong? Are you all right?"

Tiffany wasn't sure. She just wanted to get out of here, step out into the sunshine, breathe in some fresh air. She rounded a corner and ran smackdab into a nurse.

"Excuse me. I'm sorry." She met the woman's eyes . . .

Flash.

The woman was standing at a grave site. People dressed in dark colors processed by, shaking her hand and mumbling condolences. Strain pulled at the woman's tight face, and the corners of her lips trembled.

There was movement at the grave . . . the casket being lowered to the ground. The woman turned to look, and her feigned composure shattered. It was the casket of a child.

Flash.

Tiffany grabbed the wall and gaped at the woman.

"Watch out, honey!" The nurse stepped around Tiffany and went off to do her work.

Tiffany clutched her head, and leaned back against the wall. "Mom, I'm scared. Something's wrong."

"That's it! I'm getting a doctor right now." Her mother started looking around for someone to flag down.

"No. I have to get out of here." Tiffany started to run, zigzagging through the gurneys glutting the hall.

"Tiffany! Tiffany, stop!"

Tiffany stumbled to the elevators and punched the button, but the doors didn't open. She turned and headed for the exit door, then heard the elevator ring and started back.

The doors opened, and she bolted on and punched the *down* button.

"Tiffany, you stop right now!"

Tiffany ignored her mother's command. She turned to look at the well-dressed man in the elevator, and their eyes met.

Flash.

She saw him with a ski cap on his head and a gun in his hand, pointed at the convenience-store cashier. "Give me everything in the register!" The clerk didn't move fast enough, so he raised the gun and aimed it between her eyes. "Do what I say or I'll shoot!"

Flash.

Her mother stepped between her and the man, and Tiffany swallowed. Should they get off the elevator? Was the man dangerous?

"Tiffany, we are *not* leaving this hospital. Something's obviously wrong. You may be able to see, but—"

The doors opened on the first floor, and Tiffany tumbled out, her mother in tow.

"Honey, you've got to slow down. What is wrong with you?"

Tiffany's mouth twisted as she tried to hold back her fear. "Mom, something creepy is happening to me." She shoved her

46

hair back from her face and searched for the door. Why did they design these hospitals in mazes? How could anyone ever find the door?

"What, honey? Tell me what's happening."

"It's so weird. I'm seeing things that I don't really see."

Her mother grabbed her arm. "What kind of things?"

"I don't know."

She pulled her into a hug and held her, and Tiffany collapsed onto her shoulder.

"Honey, I think you're suffering from some kind of post-traumatic stress syndrome. It's very normal. You've been through an awful trauma. You may have even hit your head."

Tiffany saw the door at last and pulled herself from her mother. She started running toward it, avoiding the eyes of everyone she passed. She was going crazy . . . losing her mind. Last night she couldn't see . . . and today she couldn't *stop* seeing. She had to get out of here, into the daylight, where she knew the things spinning through her head would finally settle down.

CHAPTER EIGHT

Josh's feet were itching to go. Urgency surged through him. There was some place he needed to be, though he couldn't say exactly where. But he had the most amazing feeling. He couldn't explain it, but he was sure that if he could just start walking, his feet would take him where he needed to go . . . wherever that was.

He looked around for his father, but he'd gone to check him out. His mother had been sent home last night since the hospital was so crowded. What was taking his dad so long? They hadn't even done anything for him here, other than give him an IV with some painkillers. Why did they need massive amounts of paperwork to release someone who'd been healed by God?

His father came back into the room then, brandishing the paperwork that released Josh. "Finally, you're free to go." His dad sounded as if he'd had as much as he could take from the staff, but Josh didn't have time to think about that. He jumped up and bolted out of the room, into the crowded corridor.

"Josh! Where are you going?"

"I don't know." He knew he should wait for his father. After all, what was the hurry? But there *was* a hurry. He had to get someplace as fast as his feet would carry him. He just didn't know where that place was. He squinted as he ran, wishing he had a spare pair of glasses. His had been lost in the rubble during the quake.

He ran to the exit door, went down three flights of stairs, then out into the hall, where more people lined the walls. He zigzagged through several of the patients, then finally came to a guy lying on a gurney. Josh looked down at him and gasped. The man's face was blue.

He spun around, looking for a nurse. "Help!" he shouted. "Help! This guy can't breathe. He's turning blue. Somebody help him!"

A nurse ran to his side and screamed out, "Code blue!" All manner of alarms started to sound, and doctors ran to the man's side, pushing Josh out of the way. His father caught up to him, gasping for a breath.

"Josh, what happened? What are you doing?"

"That guy needed help." Josh twisted his face and turned back to his father. "My feet just . . . *brought* me here. It was weird."

His father took his arm and escorted him back to the elevators. "Let's get out of here. You're talking crazy. We need to get home."

Josh got onto the elevator, but that feeling came over him again. There was somewhere else he had to go. He punched the button for the ground floor, then paced the small width of the elevator car as it made its way down.

When the doors opened, he bolted out, pausing only long enough to glance back at his father. "Dad, I've got to go. I'll meet you back home later."

"No way. Your mother will be a wreck. I'm taking you home." He tried to grab Josh's arm, but Josh jerked it away. "Dad, I can't help it. Either you have to let me go, or just come with me." He went outside, then took off running—three blocks north and then another block west.

"Josh! I told you to come back here. Now! Josh!"

Josh rarely defied his father, but he didn't seem to have a choice now. His feet seemed to be in control. Josh turned a corner and saw a building that looked as if some giant foot had stomped it. A neighbor stood out in front of her own house, sweeping up debris from a fallen tree in her yard.

Squinting to bring her into focus, Josh crossed the street to her. "Ma'am, did they get everybody out of that house?"

The woman looked up at the broken structure. "It's vacant. Nobody's lived there in a year."

Josh knew better, though he didn't know how. He ran to the rubble and started digging with his hands, pulling out big sections of bricks and cement.

"Josh! Stop right now! Do you hear me?"

His father was panting and breathless when he caught up to him. "Josh, what in the world are you doing? You're acting crazy. Stop that!"

Josh *couldn't* stop. He pulled out a block of cement, a section of Sheetrock, several bricks. "Dad, there's somebody down there. Help me! Go ask that lady for a shovel." He kept digging, digging. "Can anybody hear me? Anybody in there?"

"Josh . . ." His father started to object again, but Josh held up his hand to silence him and listened. Then he heard it.

"Help me!" It was a distant, muffled voice.

"Did you hear that, Dad? There's somebody down there."

His father frowned, clearly confused. "I'll go get the shovel."

Josh dug faster, deeper, unconcerned about the skin he scraped on his hands, kicking aside the rubble and pulling up pieces of building. By the time his father was back with the shovel, the voice sounded as if it was just below him.

"I can see light. You're almost here. Help!"

"Is there anyone down there with you?"

"No. Just me."

Josh's father gaped at the hole. "Josh, how in the world did you know?"

"Got me." Josh could hardly catch his breath. "Just help me get him out."

"I'm calling an ambulance." His father pulled out his cell phone and made the call. When he hung up, he knelt beside Josh, helping him dig.

"I see you!" The man's voice was louder now, and Josh moved aside more brick, mortar, and Sheetrock.

He saw him, a man buried beneath a beam much like the one that had pinned Josh.

His father stopped him again as the sound of sirens blared toward them. "We can't move him, Josh. We have to let the paramedics do it."

Josh waited until the rescue workers got out of their units.

"There's a man buried here!" Josh yelled to the approaching men. "Hurry! I'm almost to him."

The rescue workers took over then, and in minutes they'd pulled the man from the rubble. Blood covered his tattered clothes, and he lay limp and weak as they lifted him onto the gurney.

"Thank you, son." The man's voice was raspy and hoarse, as if he'd spent the night yelling for help.

"No problem." Josh watched as they rushed him into the ambulance.

His father stared at him. "Josh, something strange is happening here."

But Josh knew he didn't have time to discuss it with his dad. His feet were moving him again.

"Josh, stop this right now! I'm warning you to stop!"

Josh looked back over his shoulder. "I can't, Pop. You've got to follow me. Come on. Hurry."

Josh took off, and soon found himself a mile or more east of where they'd found the man. He headed into a small strip mall, to a group of teenagers standing in the parking lot, smoking cigarettes and flirting.

He ran into the group, then stood there, next to a kid drinking a Coke. Urgency pulled at him again, but his feet seemed planted in this spot, like he was in the right place. But no one was buried here . . . no one's face had turned blue.

The boy looked at him, frowning. Josh felt as if he'd intruded on some kind of private moment.

"Do I know you?" The kid's voice was thick with irritation.

Some of the others turned and looked at Josh, and he felt like Steve Urkel crashing a party. But he couldn't help it! Something told him that the boy standing next to him sipping on the Coke was in trouble. He just didn't know what to do about it.

His father finally caught up to him. Josh had never seen his dad that drenched in sweat before.

"Josh—" his dad gasped the words out as he bent over, his hands on his knees—"I'm too old for this. I can't keep up with you. Now, I'm calling a cab, and we're going home immediately. Don't you move another foot!"

Josh just stood there, helpless to help the boy. What was going on? Sure, he'd awakened to healed legs—but did he also have a scrambled brain? Had the painkillers from yesterday and last night done a number on his mind?

His father put his arm around him and addressed the teens. "Josh was buried in the earthquake yesterday, at Valley High. He's a little confused."

One of the guys shrugged. "Dude, it's OK. Glad you got out, man."

A few of them reached out to slap hands with him, but Josh didn't respond. He suddenly felt very tired.

Turning away, he just let his father take him back home.

CHAPTER NINE

While Mo's mother was signing the hospital release papers, Mo introduced himself to the boy in the bed next to him.

"I was healed miraculously, like the man in the Bible who was blind and suddenly God healed him, and then the Pharisees called him in and asked him what had happened, and he didn't know, and he said, 'All I know is I was blind and now I see.'" Mo knew he was rambling, but he couldn't seem to stop himself.

"Yeah?" The weak boy in the bed seemed mildly interested.

"Yeah. Well, I wasn't blind, but my throat hurt, and I had inhaled all this smoke, and I didn't think I was ever going to be able to talk again, only God healed me . . ." The truth of his words made them come faster. "Now I just have so much to say because I feel like I need to praise Him because of what He's done."

"Uh-huh."

"Jesus is good, man. He's excellent. He's the only way, you know? Jesus is the way, the truth and the life, and no man comes to the Father but by Him. I hope you know that. Do you believe it? Are you a believer?"

The groggy man who had the bed on the other side of him sat up. "Can somebody shut him up before I scream?"

Mo hadn't expected that. "I'm sorry, sir. I was only saying that Jesus—"

Mo's mother rustled in, interrupting him. "Mo, come on out. They said we could leave."

"Good." He gathered the few things his mother had brought him from home last night and stuffed them into a duffel bag. "Mom, you realize what's happened here, don't you? I've been miraculously healed, and there must be a reason. God restored my voice, and He must want me to use it for His glory." Joy overcame him, and he held out his hands. "And I absolutely plan to do that."

She led him out of the room, and he bumped into a bed against the wall. A woman lay there, groaning. "Ma'am, I'd like to pray for you if you don't mind. See, I was healed, and the Lord who owns the universe and everything in it has that power to heal. So I'd like to pray and ask Him to send you the help you need, comfort and help with your pain."

The woman started to cry. "Get away from me."

A nurse came up behind him. "Excuse me, young man, but is there something you need?"

"I just wanted to pray for her." Mo stepped back. "I didn't

mean to upset her. But prayer is really important, because if you think about it, none of us really has any control. That earthquake yesterday really brought that home to me. That it's only my faith in Jesus Christ that makes me able to go on at all."

"Security!" the nurse shouted out. "Somebody call security!"

"Mo, you've *got* to stop talking." His mother grabbed his hand and pulled him behind her. "This is ridiculous. Come on. Let's get out of here."

"But Mama, I just feel like I have so much to say."

The small woman dragged him behind her. Though he could have hoisted her over his shoulder if he wanted, he let her pull him along.

"Don't say another word to another soul until we get out of this building. Do you understand me?"

"I'll do my best, Mama, but I just feel like I have all this stuff spilling out of me. I feel like the disciples, you know, Peter and James, who were told not to speak anymore about Christ, and they looked at the leaders and said, 'We cannot stop speaking about what we have seen and heard.' I feel exactly that way, like I have to *tell* people, and I don't know why you would stop me because all this time you've been telling me that I need to be a more serious Christian."

"It's one thing to be a serious Christian," his mother muttered as the elevator doors opened. "But your rambling is driving people crazy, Mo. You're scaring them off. I'm wondering if you need to see another doctor. There's something wrong with you."

"There's nothing wrong with me, Mama. I've never felt better in my whole life. But I just have to tell you—"

"Don't tell me anything!"

"But, Mama, the Lord—"

She held up a finger in front of his face. *"Don't!"*

"He healed—"

Her fingers snapped in front of him. "Not another word!"

As much as Mo wanted to honor his mother's wishes, he couldn't comply. So as she led him out to the car he whispered under his breath all the things that he needed to say.

CHAPTER TEN

*b*y Friday afternoon, ten members of the small community were confirmed dead in the earthquake, and fourteen were still missing. Rescue workers had kept at it around the clock, but they hadn't pulled anyone else out of the city's rubble in the last several hours. Four of the missing were from Valley High School, including the student-body vice president, the senior slated to be the valedictorian, and two band members.

When Tiffany's church called a prayer meeting for that evening, she was glad to go. She'd had all day to get over the weird visions she had seen in the hospital. Surely they'd passed by now. Besides, she wanted to see all of her friends, hug them, make sure they were all right.

And she needed to grieve over the ones who hadn't made it and the ones still lost.

The moment she and her parents walked into the big sanctuary, Sarah, one of her friends from another school, rushed up to her.

"Oh, Tiffany, I heard what happened! I'm so glad you're all right."

Tiffany looked into her eyes.

Flash.

She saw her friend sitting in a circle of teens on a living-room floor. The kid next to her burned something in a spoon he held over a candle flame. Sarah took a syringe from someone, made it suck up the liquid, then brought it to her arm and pricked it into a vein.

Flash.

Tiffany took a step back and steadied herself. So the visions weren't over. "Sarah, what have you done?"

"What?" The girl looked genuinely confused.

The reality of what she'd seen rose like the dread in her chest. "Drugs? You?"

Sarah's brows drew together, and shadows of fear darkened her eyes. "Who have you been talking to?"

Tiffany didn't know what to say. She couldn't very well tell Sarah she'd had a vision. It was . . . insane. She wanted to turn and run away, pretend she'd never seen a thing. She wanted to hide under a blanket and never look anyone in the eye again.

Sarah grabbed her arm. "Tiffany, I asked you—"

"I have to go." Tiffany slipped out of the girl's reach. "The service is about to start."

She hurried away from the girl, who stood staring after her.

Tiffany's parents followed behind her and let her pick the seat. She found a place at the back, apart from the rest of the crowd, and sat down.

How could she be so stupid? First she saw that insane vision of Sarah shooting drugs into her vein, and then what did she do? Accuse her, shake her off, and run away. But what else could she have done?

Someone tapped on her shoulder. She turned to the pew behind her and saw Sam Horrowitz, from her algebra class.

"Tiffany, I'm glad you're OK."

Flash.

She saw him as a boy, his mother standing over him, cursing flying from her mouth. "You're just like your father. You're no good, and you never will be. You won't amount to anything. I don't know why I had to be plagued with a brainless excuse for a son. I hate the day you were even born. I should have aborted you like everyone told me."

Flash.

Sam sat before her, staring at her with troubled eyes. "Tiffany, are you sure you're all right?"

Tears stung her eyes, and her mouth started to twitch. She had to get the subject off herself. "Yeah, uh, I think so. But what about you?"

"Yeah, I'm fine. I was in the library working on my term paper when it hit, and that part of the building didn't come down. We all got out OK."

The pianist began playing, and the pastor came in. Tiffany turned her misty eyes back to the cross at the front of the room. *Please don't let me see any more visions. I can't stand this,* she prayed silently. She heard voices at the door and looked back. Mo had cornered a lady, and seemed deep in intense conversation. His voice was a little louder than appropriate, but she was glad to hear that he had gotten it back.

"It was a miracle of God, you know," Mo was saying, "and I know that I was spared for a reason. I think that reason is that I'm supposed to tell as many as I can about the love of Christ because that's what the mission of every Christian is, you know. We're supposed to tell people so they'll have their eternal salvation secured, because people don't understand, you know. They just don't understand."

Mo's mother fidgeted beside him, plucking at his sleeve to make him keep walking. Tiffany looked at her own parents, who sat staring straight ahead, troubled looks on their faces. She watched Mo take a few more steps and someone else greeted him.

He started again. "You know, I think it's great we're having a prayer service tonight because this is the best place we can be because, you know, the Lord wants us to get together. He said whenever two or more are gathered in His name He's there among them, and maybe we can pray for the people who are still lost. I mean, spiritually as well as physically, and we can do something about it, you know, because that's what we're supposed to do. The church is supposed to do that."

Someone shushed him, and he brought a finger to his mouth, as if to say that he would be quiet. Tiffany watched him slip into a row of kids from their youth group. Mo started chattering again, his low voice droning on as if he had to make a speech in the time before the service started.

What had gotten into him? Mo wasn't the chattering type. He usually kept quiet, except for the sarcasm and argumentative comments that occasionally came out of his mouth. Most of the time, he acted too cool to care.

Yesterday, when they were trapped, he hadn't been able to utter a word, even to cry for help.

Her eyes widened, and her heart began to race. He must have been healed miraculously too!

Someone got up to sing a song about hope and God's control, and Tiffany closed her eyes and tried to focus on the words. But something *whooshed* past her. She looked up and saw Josh dashing by. His legs were working! Tiffany almost came to her feet, but her mother pulled her back down.

She watched, dumbstruck, as Josh trotted to the middle of the sanctuary, then hesitated. He looked from side to side, then hurried to the back again.

"His legs were crushed," she whispered to her mother. "I saw them."

Her mother followed her gaze, and they watched as Josh chose a row, then stepped over people, ignoring the empty spaces, and pushing through those who were seated. "Excuse me. Excuse me. I'm sorry." He finally came to a deacon seated on the other end of the row. He sat down next to him, staring at him. The man reached out to pat Josh's shoulder.

Suddenly, Tiffany saw a look of profound confusion pass over Josh's face. His cheeks mottled red. He muttered a few words to the man, but the man shook his head.

Josh got up and hurried the rest of the way through the row. He slipped out on the other aisle and stood there for a moment, looking dazed and confused, then dashed five rows back and stopped at a little girl just in front of Tiffany. The child looked up at him, her bottom lip puckered out as if she might burst into tears if he came one step closer.

"You're OK, aren't you?" he asked the girl. Tiffany frowned. What on earth was going on? Josh persisted. "Is there something wrong?"

The wide-eyed child shook her head, mute.

Again Tiffany saw the confusion on Josh's face. He pushed his glasses up his nose. They must be new. They didn't have the medical tape holding them together.

"You can tell me." His eyes had a frantic look now, and he knelt beside her pew. The chorus of the song from the choir loft slowed its tempo, and the congregation began to sing along.

"I know something's wrong," he insisted.

Tiffany leaned forward and touched the girl's shoulder, wanting to reassure her that Josh wouldn't hurt her. The girl jerked around, and their eyes met.

Flash.

She saw the girl digging through a garbage bin, carefully separating slimy papers. She found a wadded Burger King bag and opened it. A few French fries lay at the bottom. She grabbed them and shoved them into her mouth, cast the bag aside, and dug deeper.

Flash.

Tiffany caught her breath. The child looked clean and cared for now. Tiffany remembered when her parents had brought her into the church after adopting her. They had asked for prayers because she'd had a troubled life.

Tiffany shook the thoughts from her head. Why had she seen that vision?

Josh noticed Tiffany now. "Tiffany, you're OK!"

She started to slip out into the aisle, but before she could get to him, he turned and dashed toward the stairwell that headed up to the balcony.

Tiffany just stood there, looking in the direction he had gone, as the congregation sang another chorus.

"Honey, sit down." Tiffany's father leaned over her mother and motioned for her to take her seat. "You're disturbing the others."

Slowly she sat back down and watched the balcony. In seconds, she saw Josh heading toward the sound guy, who sat at a big table working the microphones and amplifiers. She saw Josh's mouth move . . . then that look of confusion on his face again.

She turned back to the front and stared at a spot on the pew in front of her, trying to piece it together.

The confusion on Josh's face was too familiar. Painfully familiar. It reminded her of her own confusion just that morning, when she'd seen those visions, then tonight as she'd come into this room. Mo's behavior had been strange too. She glanced at him across the sanctuary. He was whispering to the person next to him.

She saw Josh emerge from the stairwell and walk back up the aisle again. He took a seat on the end of a row, his mouth trembling as though he struggled to keep it together.

She had to talk to him. Something had happened to all three of them. Tiffany wasn't sure what, but maybe together they could figure it all out before this weirdness drove them all nuts.

CHAPTER ELEVEN

*W*hen the prayer service ended, the crowd got up and ambled out quietly, wiping tears from their faces.

Tiffany bumped into a man in the aisle. She turned to apologize, and met his gaze.

Flash.

She saw him counting out the pills that he had in his bottle, then cupping them in his hand, preparing to swallow them all.

Flash.

She turned around and started the other way, and almost tripped over a little girl, who stared up at her.

Flash.

The child lay alone in a hospital bed with no one at her side.

Flash.

The child passed, and Tiffany met an elderly man's eyes.

Flash.

The old man walked along an empty street, looking at each house, trying to remember his way home.

Flash.

Tiffany fought the panic spiraling up inside her. Her hands trembled as she pushed through the crowd, heading back toward the front of the church. She had to get to Josh and Mo.

She followed the sound of Mo's voice. He was still chattering to everyone who would listen. But no one did.

"Then the Lord showed them Himself in all the Scriptures, and I got to thinking that the only Scriptures they had yet were the Old Testament, so Jesus must be in every book of the Bible because that's what it says, isn't it? I mean—"

Tiffany reached out and touched his arm. "Mo, no one's listening to you."

He looked around. "Where's everybody going? I was just telling them—"

"I know," she said. "Please. I need to talk to you. Can you wait until I find Josh?"

"Wait." He gazed down at her. "Your eyes. They're all well. Did you have a healing too?"

"Yes, I sure did."

"Oh, man. We *do* need to talk. I'll come with you."

As they pushed through the crowd, Mo kept talking. "I'm glad you suggested this. Something weird's happening. I've never talked so much in my life. I woke up this morning and my throat and lungs were all fine. And suddenly it was like every thought in my mind had to come out through my mouth, and I can't seem to shut up. I've never been like this before."

Tiffany saw Josh darting back and forth in the crowd, as if he desperately searched for someone or something that he couldn't find. She grabbed Mo's hand and pulled him along behind her.

Flash.

A boy drowning in a lake . . .

Flash.

A girl crying as the moving van pulled away . . .

Flash.

A man doubling over with pain in his side . . .

Flash.

Tiffany tried to ignore the dizzying visions as she fought her way through the people. "Josh! Josh!" she called.

He saw her and started toward her. His face was shiny with sweat, and the expression on his face mirrored her own anxiety.

"We need to talk," he said.

"You got it. Let's go."

Mo grabbed Josh and made him turn around. "Man, you were healed too, weren't you? I didn't think I'd ever see you standing on your own feet again. Tiffany and I were healed too. Look at us! We've been marked by God somehow."

Josh shook his head. "Unbelievable."

Tiffany took both guys' hands and pulled them through the back door toward the Sunday-school rooms. She turned on the light and closed the door. Josh went straight to the window.

"Josh, what are you doing?"

He turned around to look at her and clutched his head. "I

wish I knew! I just keep feeling like I've got to go somewhere and *do* something, like there are people in trouble and I need to help them. This morning when I left the hospital, I ran past a bunch of people, then walked right up to some guy who couldn't breathe. Then I ran outside and found a man buried in the rubble of a house that everyone thought was vacant."

As he spoke, he paced rapidly across the room. "It was like my feet led me to person after person, and I knew in my gut that they were in trouble, but I couldn't figure it out when I got to them." He collapsed into a chair, clearly exhausted.

Tiffany understood, all too well. "I've had a similar thing happen. Ever since I was healed, I've been seeing visions. I don't want to, but I can't stop them. I'm seeing things I don't want to see."

Josh wiped his sweaty face on his sleeve. "Like what, Tiffany?"

"Like whenever I make eye contact with somebody, I have this . . . this *flashback* into their lives, a vision or something, where I see these horrible things happening to them. Like I see them as children getting beaten by their father or getting chewed out by their mother, or as adults having car wrecks and attempting suicide. Everything you can imagine. It's horrible, and I can't stop it. I want to help these poor people whose lives I'm seeing into, but what can I do? I can't undo their past. I don't understand what's happening."

"Man, I know just what you mean," Mo said. "I woke up this morning and my throat was clear, my lungs felt better, and next thing I know, I'm talking to everybody I see. I mean *everybody*. I've never talked to so many people in my life, and I can't seem to shut up. I just want to tell them all about Jesus and quote Scripture and testify to my healing. I'd rather shut up, but I can't—"

He stopped midsentence and clapped his hands. "All right! I'm getting a picture here." He paced to the front of the Sunday-school room. "Now it's so clear." He hit his forehead with his palm. "I don't know why I didn't think of it before."

"What are you talking about?" Josh asked.

"Well, we were all three healed, right? I mean it's obviously an act of God, a miracle, because how else could it have happened?"

"I'll buy that." Tiffany slid onto the desk in the corner of the room. "I've thought that from the beginning."

"Yeah, me too." Josh got up and slid his hands into his pockets, then began pacing the length of the room. "I mean, your legs don't just snap back into place when you've crushed the bones."

"OK, so we're healed, right?" Mo said. "But that's not all. Apparently we were healed and *then* some."

Tiffany looked up at him. "Then some . . . *what?*"

"Well, we've been given some kind of supernatural gift."

Tiffany stared at him, trying to process his words. A supernatural gift. Was that what she had?

"I mean, I'm talking Scripture like I've never talked it before. I didn't even know I knew all this stuff! And I can't stop talking about the gospel to everybody that I see. I mean, I'm driving people crazy. They're running from me left and right. Even my mother, who cried her eyes out last night at my condition, doesn't want me to say another word today. And here you are, Tiff, with this vision that you've never had before. And Josh is trying to go places where he thinks people need help. Right?"

Josh stopped his pacing. "Yeah, but why would God give us supernatural gifts that didn't *do* anything? OK, anything other than frustrate us and make us look crazy. If anything, we're running people away . . . or in my case, running from them ourselves."

Tiffany stared at the air in front of her. "Maybe God's punishing us."

"For what?" Mo asked. "What would He be punishing you for?"

"I don't know," Tiffany said. "Maybe for being a snob and not using my Christianity the way I should, for not talking to anybody about Christ . . . for just being complacent and lazy."

"Can't be." Josh slid his hands into his pockets. "Why do you think God would punish you by giving you this peek into people's lives?"

Tiffany frowned. "Well, I don't know. It doesn't *feel* like a curse. It . . . actually, it feels like I'm seeing something that only God can see, you know? Like I've been given this heavenly insight that only He has."

Josh clapped his hands. "That's it! I feel like I've got God's feet, like He knows where all the problems are and He's making my feet take me there, only I don't know what to do when I get there."

"And I feel like God gave me His mouth," Mo said, "like I'm just a mouthpiece going around preaching sermons to everybody I see, only I must be preaching to the wrong people because they don't want to hear what I have to say. I don't even know what they *need* to hear, so I'm just rambling."

Tiffany sat up straighter as understanding dawned. "Maybe we need to get our gifts in sync."

Josh and Mo both looked down at her.

"What do you mean, *in sync?*" Josh asked.

"I mean maybe we need to use them together, you know? I mean, if *you* know where to go, Josh, to find hurting people, and *I* can see their problems, then maybe *Mo* will know what to say to help them. Maybe we're supposed to be a kind of team, a helping team for hurting people. Then this stuff might make a little sense."

Josh smiled for the first time tonight, and met Mo's eyes. The linebacker started laughing.

"Oh, man!" Josh said. "Tiffany, you're making so much sense."

"Absolutely," Mo said. "In fact, the Bible tells us that we all have different gifts, and we're supposed to work together, right? That we're part of the body of Christ and that no gift is unimportant and none is more important than the other, but that if we all work together we can do miraculous things for the Lord."

"That's right," Tiffany said. "Maybe that's what God's trying to teach us, that if we work together with these supernatural gifts, well . . . we can do mighty things."

"What have we got to lose?" Mo asked. "Let's try it."

"Right now?" Tiffany hugged herself. "I don't know if I'm ready for this. It's creepy, you know, seeing into people's lives. It's freaking me out."

Mo touched her arm in an awkward attempt to comfort her. "Don't let it freak you out. Think of it as a good thing."

"Maybe it won't be weird if we're all together," Josh said. "But I've got to get out of here now. I can't be still. I can already feel my feet trying to get me to go somewhere."

"And I've got stuff to say," Mo said. "Take me to somebody who needs to hear it."

Tiffany sighed. "All right, I guess we're all in this together. One for all and all for One, like the Three Musketeers." They put their hands together, then gave each other high fives.

"Let me go tell my parents, and I'll meet you on the front steps."

"Yeah, me too," Mo said. "Five minutes."

But Josh was already up the hall.

CHAPTER TWELVE

*t*hey left the church and headed down Preston Avenue, which led to the city park. Josh walked so fast that Tiffany could hardly keep up.

"Slow down, Josh!"

"Just run," Josh said.

She shot him a disgusted look. "Run?" She pointed to her Birkenstocks. "In these shoes?"

But Josh didn't even look back, so Tiffany tried to catch up.

Mo easily kept stride with him. "This afternoon when I was at home and didn't have anybody to talk to, I started reading my Bible, and you'll never guess what God led me to."

Tiffany tripped and caught herself by grabbing onto Josh's shoulder. "I've always thought I was in pretty good shape from cheerleading and gymnastics, but I've never run track."

"Neither have I." Josh slowed down to a fast walk. "That better?"

"Yes. My feet and I thank you very much."

Mo went on. "I found these verses that didn't mean much to me at the time, but knowing what I know now, I see why God wanted me to see them."

"What were they?" Josh asked.

"In Luke 10:23 it says, 'Blessed are the eyes which see the things you see.'"

Tiffany stopped. "It says that? Oh, I've got chills."

"I know—" Mo grinned at her—"That's what I thought too. And, Josh, I found your verse."

Josh's step had sped up again, and he seemed distracted.

"Matthew 28:19. It says, 'Go therefore and make disciples of all the nations.'"

"How does that have anything to do with me?"

"*Go,* man. Don't you see? You're going. That's all you're doing, is going, going, going."

Josh turned a corner. "Yeah, I guess that's true. That could be my verse."

"And what's yours?" Tiffany was breathing hard now. "Did you find one for yourself?"

"Yeah, man, Luke 1:64. 'And at once his mouth was opened, and his tongue loosed, and he began to speak in praise of God.'"

"Cool." Tiffany felt new purpose washing over her. "God led you to those verses?"

"Of course He did. I mean, here I was, wishing I could go out and find somebody to talk to, but knowing my mama would kill me if I left the house. And I opened the Bible and turned right to those verses, one right after another."

Just then Tiffany spotted several people sitting in City Park, just ahead. A gazebo stood at the center of the park, and benches circled it. An old couple sat on one of the benches, but Josh passed them by. He headed instead toward a girl sitting alone on a bench, her feet pulled up, hugging her knees.

She was crying.

"There. That's her." Josh stopped cold. "She's the one we're supposed to come to."

"Well, why did you stop?" Tiffany gave him a little push. "We've got to go up to her."

"No, that's *your* job," Josh said. "I just bring us here. Now you have to look in her eyes and see what's wrong."

Tiffany swallowed. "But what if it doesn't work? What if I walk up to her and look like a fool?"

"You have to try, Tiffany. That's what we came for!"

She looked at the girl as if she might sprout horns and charge at them. "Okay . . . but Mo, you come with me."

"We'll all go." Mo tugged on Josh's arm. "Come on, man. Tiffany, as soon as you know the problem, let me know it somehow."

Josh got behind them, and slowly they approached the girl.

She jumped as she realized they were coming toward her. She put her feet down and grabbed the bag lying next to her, then sprang up.

Tiffany would have done the same thing if three wild-eyed kids approached her in the park. "Wait! We didn't mean to scare you."

The girl clutched her bag to her chest. "What do you want?"

Flash.

Tiffany saw her lying in the dirt. A man in a ski cap assaulted her, holding his hand over her mouth . . .

Flash.

Tiffany slapped her hand over her own mouth and stumbled back.

Mo spun around and bent down to her. "What, Tiffany? What did you see?"

"She's been raped," she whispered.

Josh's face twisted. "Tonight? Just now?"

"No. She was wearing different clothes in my vision. I don't know when it happened."

The girl seized their momentary distraction, and started to hurry away, but Mo stepped forward. "You've been hurt, haven't you, ma'am? Someone attacked you, and you don't know where to turn. Isn't that right?"

The girl swung around, her shocked eyes glistening. "How did you know that?"

"We just knew," Tiffany said.

The girl's face twisted. "People can just *look* at me and tell?"

"No, not at all. Just me."

The girl frowned, and took a step toward them.

Mo softened his voice. "Did they find the guy? Did they arrest him?"

"No." She looked so small standing there, her purse clutched against her. "I went to the police and gave them a description of him, but I don't think they've found him yet." She looked over her shoulder. "He's still out there. And I told my mother, and she said it was my fault because of what I wear. And I'm so scared, but I don't want to go home and listen to her chew me out like it's my fault." She broke down, and Tiffany rushed forward and put her arms around her.

"Please, come sit down. I'm Tiffany, and this is Josh and Mo. We need to talk to you."

The girl came willingly, and Tiffany led her over to the bench. She sat down with her, and Mo sat on the girl's other side. Josh stood in front of them.

Mo's voice became soft and gentle, and he spoke more slowly than he had since he'd been blessed with this gift. "The Bible says the Lord Jesus Christ will bind up the wounds of the brokenhearted. He can do that. What's your name?"

"Sandy," she whispered.

"He can do that, Sandy, and He sent us to tell you that. He wants you to bring what's happened to Him, and put it on His altar and let Him heal you. He's the only one who can."

The girl's hands trembled. "I really wasn't doing anything wrong. I was just walking to my dance class, and the next thing I knew, someone grabbed me and pulled me into the bushes." She sucked in a sob, her face conveying the terror in her words.

Mo spoke with gentle authority. "The Lord will avenge what's happened to you. All you can do right now is trust Him."

"It's like the earthquake brought out the worst in every-body!" Sandy looked at Tiffany. "I don't understand it. We should all be bonding together, trying to help each other. But, no, there are people out there looting, breaking into stores, stealing things. It's like the worst of humanity came out, and people ran everywhere and . . . and this guy . . . he just came out of nowhere."

"Where were you when the earthquake hit?" Mo asked.

"In my car, on a bridge. I felt it swaying. I just knew it was going to collapse, but it didn't. When I got off of there, I thought I'd escaped the disaster. But then something even worse happened. I wish I'd died on the bridge!"

"Sandy, you survived for a reason. The Lord loves you and wants you for His own. He sent us to tell you."

"I want that," she said. "I really do. I've studied Zen Buddhism and Eastern religions. I almost became a Hare Krishna. I even read the Koran and tried to see if that would fit my life . . . but none of it did."

"Christ is the only way." Mo's words brooked no debate. "He's the way, the truth, and the life. No man can come to the Father except through Him. It's like, if you wanted to get into a really great concert, you'd have to have a ticket or something, right? But if you don't have a ticket, you have to know the right person to get in. If you know somebody who's, say, in the band, you can go right in, get treated like royalty, enjoy the benefits of being a friend. But you don't get in because of who *you* are. You get in because of who you *know*. It's that way with Jesus.

We can't get into heaven through Buddha or Hare Krishna or Islam . . . only through Jesus. If we know Him, we'll get in."

The girl had stopped crying and her gaze riveted on Mo. "How do I do it? How can I know Jesus? How can I start His healing?"

Tiffany's heart leaped. She hadn't expected for the girl to be so compliant, so willing to grasp onto the life jacket they threw her.

"Just pray," Mo said. "Ask Him for it."

"We can pray with you," Tiffany offered.

The girl nodded. "Yes, that would be good. I've never done this before." Sandy bowed her head and started to pray in a shaky, awkward voice. As she did, Tiffany's soul stirred with a wonder she had never known. She'd never witnessed anyone coming into the kingdom, and she certainly hadn't played a part in getting anyone there before.

Gratitude swelled in her heart as the girl poured out her heart to the Lord.

No doubt about it, these gifts were not accidental. They were for a purpose. God's purpose. And Tiffany couldn't wait to see where they took her next.

When they had walked Sandy to her home, Josh turned on Tiffany and Mo. "We took too long with her. There were other places we needed to go. We couldn't afford to spend that much time on one person."

Tiffany couldn't believe he could find fault with what they'd done. "Josh, what's gotten into you? We *had* to stay with her. What did you want us to do, say amen and then hit the road?"

"I've been given the gift to *go,* not to stay," Josh said. "There were other places we needed to be."

"You're out of your mind," Mo said. "The Bible said go and *disciple*. We're not supposed to just talk to people and then abandon them. We have to do something afterward."

"I'm just saying there are other people who need us." Josh started walking away, but Tiffany stopped him.

"Josh, I'm tired. I need to go home. It's almost midnight. My mother is probably worried sick."

Josh waved her off. "Okay, go. Mo and I can handle it."

"No, man!" Mo dug in, refusing to follow him. "We can't do it without her. You'll just get us to the place where there's a need, and I'll just start talking randomly, and neither one of us will know what the real problem is."

Tiffany saw the frustration on Josh's face and she understood. But the fact remained that she needed to get home. "We can start out again tomorrow. It's Saturday, so we can work all day if you want to. I'm going to go visit Sandy again as soon as I get up. I want to make sure she's all right. Then I'll meet you guys somewhere."

Clearly Josh didn't like it, but he gave a resigned sigh. "All right. Just call us when you get up. I'll be raring to go." He looked at Mo. "You and I could still try, you know."

"Man, Tiffany's right. It's nearly midnight. I've got a curfew, man."

"Oh, so you're bailing on me too? Come on, Mo. You probably haven't met curfew all year."

"I'm not *bailing*. I'm just saying that Tiffany has a point. We've been through a lot the last couple of days, and my folks are probably climbing the walls waiting for me too. It's really late. We're still supposed to honor our parents, with or without these Superman gifts."

Josh looked at his watch, and his cheeks reddened in the light of the streetlamp. "Aw, you're right. By now my father has probably called out the National Guard and threatened to sue every one of them."

Tiffany smiled.

"Look," Mo said, "let's just go home and get a good night's sleep. We'll wait for Tiffany to call us in the morning; then we can head out again."

Josh finally gave in. "All right, I guess."

Tiffany breathed a sigh of relief. "Anybody want to walk me home?"

"We both will," Mo said. "Then we'll crash for the night."

They were all quiet as they headed to Tiffany's neighborhood, just a few blocks from the church. Mo had grown quiet, and Josh's step seemed heavier and slower than it had been all day.

When they got to her house, she went inside, headed for her room, and fell into bed, more exhausted than she'd ever been in her life.

CHAPTER THIRTEEN

Saturday morning, Tiffany met the guys at Josh's house. They were glued to the television when his mother let her in. She rustled into the living room.

"You guys aren't gonna believe this. I found Sandy reading her Bible this morning. Isn't that great?"

But neither of them took their eyes from the tube.

"Look—" Mo nodded to the live television coverage of what used to be their school—"They found the four missing kids."

Tiffany sucked in a breath and sat down. "Are they alive?"

"They found Alex Shepherd and Lana Gray alive. Guy Mason and Evan Turner didn't make it."

Tiffany slowly brought her hands to her mouth as she sank onto the couch. She listened in a half daze as images of the two dead boys drifted through her mind. She had seen Guy in French class the morning of the earthquake. He'd been laughing and goofing off, like any other day.

Evan Turner had led the Drug-Free assembly just the day before.

A question, cruel and accusing, floated through her mind. Why hadn't she ever taken the time to find out if either of them were Christians?

When the coverage ended, Josh wiped his eyes. "I feel like such a jerk."

"Why?" Mo asked.

"Because I had classes with both of those guys. I never shared my faith with them. I never cared about their souls at all."

Mo swallowed. "We all thought we had all the time in the world."

Tiffany just stared. "We were wrong."

Josh sat there a moment, rubbing his eyes. Finally, he got to his feet. "Well, we know better now."

"Yeah." Mo stood. "We better get out there."

Tiffany followed as he said good-bye to his mother then led them out the door. Somber and pensive, she and Josh trailed him out of his neighborhood, without a clue where they were heading.

They were quiet as Josh led them through the quake-marred town. Here and there a wall had come down, a building had collapsed. Fissures crossed streets like newly dug ditches. Tiffany whispered a prayer of thanks that more people had not been killed.

Josh's feet led them to the mall, straight into a department store, through the fragrance and makeup counters and into the men's department. It seemed wrong, somehow for business to go on as usual when grief cloaked the town. But the store's piped-in music still played softly and cheerily, and perfume wafted on the air, as if death hadn't knocked on the door. As if hundreds didn't lie in the hospital just a few blocks away.

Undaunted by the weird normalcy, Josh hurried up to a counter, as if the store was about to close and he had one last purchase to make.

The clerk, a young man of about nineteen or twenty, smiled up at them. "May I help you?"

Flash.

Tiffany saw him walking up a sidewalk, skipping a few steps onto the porch, opening the front door. He burst inside . . . and stopped cold at the sight of his father embracing a woman at least twenty years younger than his mother.

Flash.

The clerk still waited . . . smiling. . . .

Tiffany's mind went blank. "Uh . . . excuse me . . . just a minute . . . OK?"

"Sure. My name's Mike. I'll be right here if you need me."

Tiffany stepped away from the counter, and Mo bent down. "Tell me, Tiff."

She glanced back at Mike. He had taken an armful of clothes and was loading them onto hangers. "Poor guy walked into his house and found his father making out with a girl."

Mo winced. "That's gotta hurt."

Tiffany, Josh, and Mo went back to the counter, and before

Mike knew what hit him, Mo had struck up a conversation about disappointment, betrayal, and deception. Tiffany listened, amazed. Mo hadn't only been given the gift of speaking . . . he'd also been given a sensitivity that he hadn't had before. He knew what to say and exactly how to say it. Mike hung on every word, his gaze riveted on Mo's as they talked.

Finally Mike took a break and sat down with them at the food court, where Mo told him about the unchanging Lord who heals our wounds and returns the years that the locusts ate.

By the time Mike went back to work, he had offered his life up to Christ.

Tiffany's joy weighed heavily on her heart, and she couldn't seem to hold back her tears. *I haven't done a thing, Lord, to deserve this privilege . . . watching people give their lives to you . . . being a part of your Holy Spirit's work.*

But here she was, right in the middle of all of it, simply responding to the gift she'd been given.

She hoped she didn't blow it.

When they were finished, Mike promised to meet them at the gazebo in City Park tomorrow. From there they would take him to church so he could worship his newfound Lord.

CHAPTER FOURTEEN

*W*hen they left the mall, Tiffany followed the guys, glad she'd worn running shoes today. They went about a mile up the road, to a strip mall that looked as if the earthquake had missed it completely.

Josh's step slowed as they reached the parking lot.

Tiffany looked around. "What is it, Josh?"

"That guy over there. See him?"

Tiffany followed his gaze. Josh had to be kidding! The kid he pointed to wore gang colors, a backward baseball cap on his head, and gloves with the fingers cut out. He smoked a cigarette as he paced back and forth in front of a store window.

"No way I'm approaching him!" She spun to stare at Josh. "That guy's obviously a gang member."

"He's the one God led me to," Josh said. "You have to look in his eyes. Tell us what the deal is."

"God wouldn't have led you to *him!*"

"Why not?" Mo whispered.

"Because he's dangerous, that's why. I recognize those colors. That gang is responsible for a lot of bad things in this town."

"I'm telling you, *he's* the one," Josh said. "Now are you going to be obedient, or not?"

"I don't have to be obedient to you."

"I'm talking about obedience to *God*. Jesus died for that guy too."

She knew he was right. God probably had led Josh's feet to this boy. She drew in a deep breath. Trembling, she stepped forward, and as the guy turned around, their eyes met.

Flash.

He sat in a dark room lit only by candles. Guys with tattoos and switchblades walked back and forth in front of him. One guy stopped in front of him, slapped the back of his blade on his palm. "Dante, my man . . . your initiation is to off somebody. You tell us who it's gonna be, and we watch for their obit in the paper. That way, you can't go picking some guy who died of natural causes and claim you killed him."

The others laughed.

"'Off somebody?' Who?"

"Anybody. You pick."

Dante gaped up at him, clearly not sure he heard right. "We talking murder?"

"We all had to do it too," he said. "When we see the obit, you're in, man."

Flash.

Tiffany felt the blood seep from her face. She turned around. Mo and Josh leaned in, waiting to hear what she had seen. She shook her head and pushed past them, and didn't stop walking until she was a block away.

Josh and Mo caught up to her. "Tiffany, what's wrong?" Mo asked. "What did you see?"

She spun around. "He's a killer, that's what!"

"A killer?"

"It's his gang initiation. He's been ordered to kill somebody, and he can pick anybody he wants. And the way he's walking in front of that store and looking inside, I'm worried. His name's Dante."

"Ah, man. Let me at him." Mo took off, calling back over his shoulder, "We didn't come a minute too soon."

Tiffany watched Mo bolt up the sidewalk, but she and Josh hung back. She heard him starting his conversation. At first the guy didn't look interested, but finally his eyes connected with Mo's, and Tiffany was surprised to see only respect and attention on his face. They stood like that, talking quietly for over half an hour.

Tiffany and Josh leaned against a store's outside wall, watching as Mo used his gift.

"I still say this is a waste of time. No way a hardhearted guy like that is going to listen to the gospel."

"God doesn't make mistakes, Tiffany," Josh said. "He knows what he's doing."

"You're sure he's the one God led you to?"

"Absolutely."

She sighed and leaned back against the wall, watching as Mo grew animated, obviously preaching to the kid. She couldn't believe the guy hadn't already bashed Mo in the head and taken his wallet. But the kid just stood there, listening to every word.

Finally, the boy broke into tears and covered his eyes with those half-gloved hands.

"Look at that." Josh's tone rang of I-told-you-so.

"Yeah, I see." She couldn't hide the disappointment in her voice. It wasn't fair. Someone like that needed to be locked up, not showered with the same grace God had given her . . .

Josh pushed off from the wall. "Come on, Tiff. Maybe we need to go help Mo out."

"No." She grabbed his arm. "I think Mo's handling it on his own. He's doing fine."

Josh shoved his glasses up on his nose. "We're a team, Tiffany. He's a human being, and we're supposed to love him too."

"But look what he was about to do. That he'd even *consider* something like that—"

"He hasn't done it. Mo stopped him, and now we've got to help do the rest."

She looked up the street. "But what if his friends come? What if they attack us and drag us away? Sandy was right. This earthquake has brought out the worst in people."

"It's also brought out the best." Josh breathed a laugh. "Take us, for instance."

Tiffany just stared at him, troubled. "I guess you're right."

"Come on, Tiffany. We have work to do."

Mo introduced Josh and Tiffany, and Dante shook their hands. "Dudes, you don't know what perfect timing you have. I was just about to do something that woulda ruined my life forever."

Josh sent Tiffany a look. "God must have intervened."

"Oh, He did, man. He did. You know, I heard about Jesus when I was a kid. My grandmother, she was devout. On her knees all the time. Dragged me to church every time the doors opened. But then I hooked up with these homeboys, and I wanted to be a part of the group, you know what I'm saying? I wanted to belong somewhere."

Tiffany hadn't expected to relate to the boy, but she did. She'd felt those same things. "What are you going to do now?"

Dante looked down at the concrete, contemplating his future.

"You can't go back to that gang," Mo told him. "Man, you have to stay away from those guys."

"I know what you're saying. But I'm thinking they need to know what I know. How will they know about God unless somebody tells them? We had two brothers killed yesterday in the quake. Dudes are starting to think about what if *they* had died. Maybe wondering whose side they should be on. Satan's or God's. We've mostly been on Satan's side, but I'm not so sure they want to stay on that side now that everything's happened, you know what I'm saying? So I've got to go back there. I've got to tell them what you just told me. If they don't want to listen . . . then I'll move on."

Josh straightened and lifted his chin. "We'll come with you."

Tiffany caught her breath and seared Josh with a look. Had he gone completely nuts?

"You would, man?" Dante asked. "You'd go with me, knowing they got knives and guns and can be mean as the devil hisself?"

Tiffany wobbled and had to reach out to steady herself. She was going to faint. She knew it.

But Josh's feet were already moving. Tiffany looked to Mo, pleading for help, but he just shrugged and grinned. "The LORD is my light and my salvation," he said. "Whom shall I fear? The LORD is the stronghold of my life—of whom shall I be afraid?"

"OK, man, let's go." Dante took off down the sidewalk, Josh right beside him. Mo was close on their heels.

Tiffany fell into step beside Mo, but touched his arm to get his attention. "Mo, this is crazy." She mouthed the words so Dante couldn't hear.

Mo shook his head. "'When evil men advance against me to devour my flesh, when my enemies and my foes attack me, they will stumble and fall.' You hear that, Tiff? Stumble and fall."

She held her hands out to show him how badly she trembled. Dante looked back over his shoulder, then turned around, walking backward. "You dudes don't have to come, you know. I don't blame you if you don't want to."

She opened her mouth to tell him that she needed to get home, but Mo spoke instead.

"'Though an army besiege me, my heart will not fear; though war break out against me, even then will I be confident.' Psalm 27:1–3." Mo grinned. "You can do this, Tiffany."

She gulped back the lump in her throat and prayed that those verses would apply to them.

Dante led them to an old, abandoned house on the bad side of town. *Protect us, Lord. Please protect us.*

She tried to be strong, but the fear seemed to have frozen her muscles. She had survived an earthquake, only to walk into this? It was insane, reckless.

She hung back as Dante stepped inside. Quickly, he returned. "Man, they ain't here."

Tiffany let out a ten-pound breath. *Thank You, Lord.*

But Josh wasn't daunted. His feet already seemed to be moving him away from the house. "I know where they are."

"What?" Dante asked. "How would *you* know?"

"Just follow me."

"But you don't know them—"

"God does." Josh walked faster, then cut through a yard between two broken-down, dilapidated houses. He cattycornered through the backyard, then came out on another street.

Tiffany was sweating by the time he led them into the woods behind the houses, down to the edge of a smelly creek. She jerked to a halt as she saw the gang congregated around a small fire, some of them sitting on a fallen log, the rest on the ground. A huge guy—maybe six foot five and 250 pounds—

got up as Tiffany and the guys approached. He looked as though he could break her in half with little effort.

"'The LORD is my light and my salvation,'" she whispered. "Whom shall I fear? The LORD is my light and my salvation . . . whom shall I fear? The LORD. . . '"

Their eyes met.

Flash.

She saw him watching a couple as they crossed a street. His step picked up, and he came up behind them. The man looked over his shoulder and started to walk faster. The girl broke into a run, and the gang member descended on her, grabbing her up like a child, muffling her mouth with his huge hand.

"Scream and you're dead," he hissed out. "Give me your wallets."

The girl swallowed back her scream and thrust her purse at him. The man tossed him his wallet and grabbed the girl. The two took off running . . .

Flash.

Tiffany spun around, away from the hulk coming toward them. "Mo, I saw him assaulting a couple. He's dangerous. Please, can we go?"

But Mo made no move to leave. He only stood straighter and walked to stand beside Dante.

Four hours later, two more gang members had given their lives to Christ. The mugger in her vision, who called himself Ripper after the famed serial killer, was one of them.

But as Tiffany watched, the huge, hardened gang member wilted like a weary lamb.

"I done some bad things, man. Some real bad things. If God can wash me clean, man, then I owe Him everything." His face twitched with the weight of his grief. "I got up this morning and I told the Lord that if He was true, if He was really real, that He would send somebody to help me, that He would prove who He was. And that's what He did today, man. You dudes, you came here knowing what we was like, but you took the chance. And I know without a doubt that God sent you."

They heard a siren from a distance, and Tiffany peered through the trees. A blue light flashed through.

"Cops, man!" One of the gang jumped up. "We got to get out of here."

A mad scramble ensued as most of the gang members grabbed their weapons and scattered into the woods.

Dante and Ripper didn't move. "I ain't going nowhere, man," Ripper said. "I'm staying right here. They can come and get me."

Tiffany's voice was weak and hoarse. "Is it you they're after?"

"Probably. I been causing a lot of trouble around town." He got up and kicked his foot through some rotting leaves. "Didn't even bother me 'til now." He wiped the tears from his face. "Man, how can God even look at me?"

Tiffany forgot her fear for a moment as her heart ached for him. She took a step toward him and touched his back. "God *can* look at you. And what He sees is a dearly loved son, coming home."

The sirens stopped, and Tiffany heard car doors slamming.

Within seconds, police had surrounded the place where they stood, and as the officers closed in, Ripper put his hands on top of his head. "I'm here. It's me you want," he shouted. "Leave these others alone. They didn't do nothing!"

Tiffany, Josh, and Mo stood back as the police snapped cuffs on Ripper's arms, then loaded him into the backseat of the squad car. Dante sat in another car, with a couple of the other gang members the officers had rounded up, answering questions.

Before they closed Ripper in, he yelled out, "God will help me through all this, 'cause I'm a new man now. Ain't that right?"

"That's right!" Mo moved closer to the car. "You're a new man."

The police closed the back door, and the car began to pull away. Tiffany and the guys watched as the police closed the other car door. Dante flashed them a thumbs-up as that car pulled out of sight too.

Tiffany, Mo, and Josh stood in the street, staring in the direction the cars had gone.

"Wow," Tiffany said. "I can't believe this."

"Man, three gang members met Christ today." Mo's voice came out low, reverent. "Who would have thought?"

"Not me," Tiffany said. "If it had been up to me, I'd have never come to this part of town."

"Me neither." Josh laughed softly. "I'm not exactly known

for my courage. At five-four, I don't make for much of a threat. But my feet have courage . . ."

"And my eyes do," Tiffany said.

"And so does my mouth." Mo grinned at them. "Man, two days ago, you couldn't have paid me enough to preach a sermon to guys like that. I wouldn't have even known what to say."

"God's really done a number on us."

Josh started walking, but Tiffany hung back, not in much of a hurry to leave. She had dreaded coming to this part of town, but now that she was here, she felt as though she stood on holy ground. God was in this place, and she had been a witness to His mighty work today. Once again she felt the sweet privilege of being a part of that work . . . and the overwhelming gratitude that she hadn't let her fear rob her of it.

CHAPTER FIFTEEN

*t*iffany and Mo followed Josh back across town, each of them lost in their own thoughts about what had just taken place. When Tiffany's cell phone rang, she dug it out of her purse and flipped it open.

"Hello?"

"Tiffany, it's Sandy. I was wondering if I could go to church with you tomorrow. I don't have a church, and I don't even know where to start looking for one. Since I already know three people—"

Tiffany laughed. "Of course you can come to church with us." She winked at the others, and Josh and Mo high-fived. "I tell you what. I'll meet you at City Park right in the gazebo at nine o'clock tomorrow morning. How does that sound?"

"Really good." Sandy's relief was evident. "I'll be there."

Tiffany clipped the phone shut, and punched the air. "Sandy's coming to church."

"We need to invite the others too," Mo said. "We need to get them all there."

Josh started walking again. "I hope the church is ready for this, because we're going to need their help. We can't disciple these people by ourselves, but like you said, we can't just abandon them."

"That's how it *should* work." Excitement shone on Mo's face. "Every part of the Body working to do his or her special job, everyone with a different gift. That's what the Bible says ought to happen. That's what church is all about, right?"

"But no one has gifts like ours," Tiffany said. "They only have teaching and hospitality and stuff."

"Come on, there are a lot more gifts than that," Mo said, "and they're all supernatural if you think about it. I mean, when you have the Holy Spirit, don't you naturally have the gifts?"

Tiffany breathed a laugh. "You would think so. Only I never used mine before. I'm not even sure what gifts I had."

"Well, maybe you never used them because you never felt they were needed. But tomorrow the people at the church are going to find out how needed they are."

CHAPTER SIXTEEN

*t*iffany's alarm clock blared at six the next morning. She had set it to wake her early, so she could pray and study the Scriptures, in hopes of being ready for whatever the Lord lay before her today.

She needed strength—physically, emotionally, and spiritually—to help their new sisters and brothers in Christ.

Tiffany opened her Bible and looked down at it, chewing her lip. Where should she start reading? She'd never been one to spend a lot of time poring over Scripture, but now she felt it was a missing piece in her life. A much-needed piece for the job she had before her.

But what if it was too late to catch up? In many ways, it was as if the Lord had given her a job to do, but she had flippantly skipped the training.

She flipped to Romans, turned a few pages, and then her eyes fell to a highlighted passage: Romans 12. Brother Jim, her pastor, had preached on this last week, just days before the earthquake. His sermon had been about equipping the Body of Christ . . . how each person had a different gift, and all those gifts worked together.

She caught her breath as she realized how appropriate a passage it was for her to read today. It was no coincidence that she had turned to this chapter.

Hungry for the message buried on the page, she began to read.

. . .

Josh woke before dawn and sat upright in bed, looking around. Was God about to move his feet again? He got up, his bare feet cold on the hardwood floor. He groped for his glasses, shoved them on, then scratched his head and crossed his bedroom.

His Bible lay open on his computer desk, and he glanced down to see a passage he had outlined in pencil just last week. He turned on his lamp and slowly began to read from Romans 12.

> *I urge you, therefore, brethren by the mercies of God, to present your bodies a living and holy sacrifice, acceptable to God, which is your spiritual service of worship.*
>
> *And do not be conform to this world, but be transformed by the renewing of your mind.*

Josh stopped reading and set his chin on his palm. He stared at a nail hole in his wall, running those last few words

TERRI BLACKSTOCK

through his mind. *Transformed by the renewing of your mind.* What did that mean?

The answer came to him like a whisper, so clear and concise that he knew it must be from God. "Duh!" Josh said out loud. "He means that just because your feet are running all over the place doing cool things for God, it doesn't mean you're hot stuff. More than your feet needs to change."

He looked down at the page and read on.

> *That you may prove what the will of God is, that which is good and acceptable and perfect. For through the grace given to me I say to every man among you not to think more highly of himself than he ought to think; but to think so as to have sound judgment as God has allotted to each a measure of faith.*

Josh got up and looked at himself in the mirror. He still looked like a nerd. On one side of his head, his bed hair stuck out in every direction. On the other side, it was matted down. His glasses looked thicker than the windshield on his father's car, and he was so short the school bullies could stuff him into his own locker.

Even so, he was chosen by God, and not just to have amazing feet. He met his gaze in the mirror, and stood up straighter. After all those years of being the last man chosen for the PE teams he'd been forced to play on, God had chosen *him* for salvation, and eternal life, and a share in Christ's own inheritance. He'd never be the last man picked again. Instead

102

he was a starter on *the* winning team. He went back to his
Bible and read on.

> *For just as we have many members in one body and all the*
> *members do not have the same function, so we, who are many, are*
> *one body in Christ, and individually members one of another.*

"Whoa." Josh stepped back. It was no random act that he
had just read this passage. The Lord was speaking to him.

· · ·

Mo hadn't slept at all. He had stayed up all night reading
Scripture and trying to prepare himself for the situations the
Lord would put him in today. It was almost six when he came
to Romans 12.

> *And since we have gifts that differ according to the grace*
> *given to us, let each exercise them accordingly: if prophecy,*
> *according to the proportion of his faith, if service, in his serv-*
> *ing; or he who teaches, in his teaching; or he who exhorts, in*
> *his exhortation; he who gives, with liberality; he who leads,*
> *with diligence; he who shows mercy, with cheerfullness.*

Mo set the Bible down, as if it had burned his hands, and
scooted his chair back from the table. "Why did you show me
this, Lord?"

He got up and walked around the kitchen, stretching and

thinking. "We've got these gifts and we've used them together... But there are other gifts, and other gifted people . . ."

His voice trailed off, and he picked the Bible back up.

> *Let love be without hypocrisy. Abhor what is evil; cling to what is good. Be devoted to one another in brotherly love; give preference to one another in honor; not lagging behind in diligence, fervent in spirit, serving the Lord.*

The Lord was showing him that their work didn't stop when they "closed the deal" by leading someone in the sinner's prayer. There was more to be done. Lots more.

"Teach me, Lord," Mo said out loud.. "I'm listening."

CHAPTER SEVENTEEN

*J*osh and Mo were already waiting at the gazebo when Tiffany made it to City Park. As she cut across the grass, she saw Sandy Miller getting out of her car. She had three girls with her.

Tiffany met her halfway and hugged her, while Mo and Josh came up behind her. "You almost beat me here. How are you doing?"

"I'm good. Feeling better every day. I hope it's all right that I brought some friends. Liz Moore, Kate Anderson, and Sharon Wright."

Tiffany smiled and welcomed each of the girls. "I'm so glad you came."

"We're waiting for some others," Mo said. "Soon as they're all here, we'll head over to the church."

Sandy pulled Tiffany aside. "My friend Liz is bulimic. She really needs help. I was hoping you or somebody could talk to her today. It might make a difference."

Tiffany glanced back at the thin girl, who was laughing and

talking to Mo. She wondered why she hadn't had a flash when she met Liz. "Sure. I've never had an eating disorder, myself, but I have a good friend in Sunday school who was hospitalized last year. She was bulimic too, and she almost died because she got real dehydrated from purging. She's doing a lot better now. Maybe I could introduce them."

"That would be great."

They rejoined the group, and Tiffany saw Mike, the clerk from the department store, pulling into a parking space beside the park. He, too, had brought friends. As they got out of the car, she counted five people with him. She couldn't imagine how he'd gotten all of them into his little Civic.

He joined them in the gazebo. "Hope you don't mind that I brought a few of the guys with me."

"No, man." Mo shook his hand. "It's *great*." He turned to Mike's friends. "I'm Mo, and this is Josh and Tiffany. Sandy, Liz . . ." His voice trailed off as he came to the last two of Sandy's friends.

"Kate and Sharon," Sandy provided.

"Yeah. Kate and Sharon."

Tiffany glanced at Mo. There was an odd note in his voice, as if he was uncertain or even embarrassed. Tiffany waited for the words to pour out, but he just stood there, his hands in his pockets. What on earth . . . ? Surely he wasn't trying to find something to say? Not talk-a-mile-a-minute Mo?

Finally he looked at Mike and the others. "So . . . here we all are."

Tiffany frowned. Mo hadn't been awkward with words since the healing, but now . . . he seemed to struggle with how to make conversation.

She looked at the guys who'd just come up with Mike. Her eyes connected with one. She waited for the flash, but again nothing happened.

Her gaze shot to Josh. He was leaning against a post on the gazebo, staring down at his feet. They were still.

Something was wrong.

She stepped over to him and nudged him. "You OK?"

"Yeah. Just thinking."

She started to ask him about what when the sound of motorcycles came roaring around the corner. Dante and four of his buddies pulled up onto the lawn, then rode right up to the gazebo. Sandy and her friends seemed to draw closer together.

Leaving the bikes idling, Dante came to slap Mo's hand. "We goin' to church, or what?"

Mo laughed. "We're going to church." He looked around and apparently decided everyone was here. He glanced back at Dante. "You taking the bikes over or you want to leave them here?"

Dante turned his ignition off and stomped down his kickstand. "We'll leave them here and walk with you. It ain't far." He got off the bike and raked his fingers through his hair. "Man, I brought some of my boys with me. That OK?"

"Sure," Mo said. "What happened last night when the police took you in?"

"A brother bailed me out. I go to court next month. You'll pray for me, won't you?"

"Of course we will," Josh said.

The gang members got off of their bikes, then locked them together. Sandy and her friends looked frightened, so Tiffany went to stand with them. "Last night Dante and a couple of his friends gave their lives to Christ. I was there. I know it was real, so you don't have to be afraid."

Sandy just swallowed and nodded.

"Hey, I need a favor," Dante said as he shrugged out of his jacket. He wore a dress shirt and jeans, not the gang colors that he'd been wearing the day before.

"What's that?" Josh asked.

"My grandmother, she lives by herself. She's eighty and real poor. And I think she needs some help. Her roof is leaking, and the house is in bad shape. And I don't think she's eating real good."

"Do you want us to go see her?" Mo asked.

"Could you, man? Today, I mean? It would mean a lot to me."

"Sure," Mo said. "We'll go after the service. OK, guys?"

"Of course," Josh said. "Sure, we can do that. No problem." He looked a little preoccupied as he looked at Tiffany.

"Sure," Tiffany said. "Right after church."

As they crossed the street and walked down to the church, Tiffany glanced into each of their eyes. Nothing happened.

It was as if there was nothing to see in any of these seekers, but she knew that couldn't be true. Why couldn't she see the visions?

She looked ahead to Mo, who led the group with his hands in his pockets. He was eerily quiet. And behind them, Josh lagged behind, his brows pleated as if he tried to work out something in his mind.

Yes . . . something was very wrong.

When they reached the church, Jerry, their youth minister, made a fuss over the visitors. Before Sandy and Mike and the others knew it, they had all been swallowed into the crowd of Christians waiting to welcome them.

Mo stood back, leaning against the wall, a disturbed look on his face. Josh sat slumped in a chair, staring at his feet. Tiffany kept meeting the eyes of those around her, but there were still no flashes.

Finally, she grabbed Josh's hand and pulled him to his feet. "Come with me."

He came willingly, and she led him to Mo. "We've got to talk. In the hall."

Mo followed her without comment, and when they'd reached the hall, she turned around and faced both guys.

"OK, what's going on?"

"What do you mean?" Mo asked.

"I mean you're not talking, Mo, and Josh, you're not walking."

"I know." Josh's eyebrows shot up. "Something's happened."

"To me too," Tiffany said. "I haven't had a vision all day."

Mo just stood there, hands on his hips. "Do you think we've lost it? The gifts, I mean?"

Tiffany threw up her hands. "Why? Why would God take the gifts away when we've just started using them? We've had them how long? Two days? What was the point if they weren't going to last?"

"I don't get it." Josh shoved his glasses up on his nose. "Maybe we didn't use them well enough. Maybe we failed Him somehow."

"No way!" Mo said. "Look what God did with the gifts. Why would He be mad at us?"

"But I'm such a wimp," Tiffany said. "Yesterday, I was so afraid of that gang, even when you kept telling me that God was in control, that I had no one to fear."

"Hey, stop beating yourself up," Josh said. "You went through with it, scared or not. And look what happened this morning. They're here, aren't they?"

"There you guys are!"

They all turned and saw Jerry, the youth minister, standing in the doorway. "I was looking for you. I wanted you to give your testimonies, about being buried and rescued and healed." He grabbed Mo's arm. "Mo, you go first."

Mo stiffened. "I can't. I don't know what to say."

"Just tell them what happened to you, man. Come to think of it, all three of you go up together. You're a team, right? Tell them how fifteen people ended up coming with you to church this morning."

Slowly, the three followed him into the room. Tiffany looked around at the expectant faces. She moved to the podium and looked out. Sandy Miller was there, deep in conversation with one of the teachers, who listened with tears in her eyes. Sandy's friend Liz was sitting with Caroline Cox, the girl who'd almost died of bulimia.

Across the room, Mike stood in the corner with Jason Smith, whose parents had recently divorced. And Dante sat at a table near the opposite wall, where one of the Sunday school teachers showed him something in the Bible.

"I don't think we failed." Josh spoke from beside her. "Look at them. We started things off, but the church is doing the rest."

Mo nodded. "He's right. I didn't know how to talk to Dante today, but Mr. Sanford does. He used to be a gang member in Philadelphia. And who could help Mike better than another kid who's seen his home ripped apart?"

Jerry got everyone's attention, and all eyes turned to the front of the room, where the trio stood. "A couple of days ago, our three friends here were buried under two floors of their school. I don't have to tell you that I was praying like crazy for them. They were pulled from the rubble, alive, but badly injured. I'm going to let them tell you about their miraculous healings, and how it motivated them to share the love of Christ. Give it up, guys, for Tiffany, Josh, and Mo."

Applause sounded over the room, and the three stood there, staring at each other. She couldn't do it. She couldn't speak to this crowd. Jerry would just have to understand.

But as she turned to leave, Mo took the mike. "Well . . . uh . . . the thing is . . . before two days ago, I was kind of a selfish Christian." He cleared his throat, adjusted the mike, looked around at the faces. "I kept it all to myself. Didn't pray much. Hardly ever read the Bible, except here at church. And then something happened. I breathed a bunch of smoke and wrecked my vocal chords. My lungs were messed up, my throat was blistered . . . I didn't know if I'd ever talk again. And I got to thinking how I'd wasted my voice, and how I might not ever have another chance to use my mouth for God. But God decided to heal me."

The group erupted into loud applause, and Mo turned back to Josh and Tiffany. In a low voice that only they could hear, he said, "We're *still* healed, you know. God may have taken the gifts away, but He didn't take the healing."

Tiffany let those words sink in. The gift was gone . . . but the healing remained. What did that mean?

A slow smile crept over Josh's face. Shoving his glasses up on his nose, he took the microphone. "I was pinned under part of a wall and some kind of steel beam. My legs were all crushed and mangled. I'll be honest. I thought I was gonna die. The pain was pretty fierce. The doctors said my femur was crushed. It looked bad. And then the next morning, like Mo, I woke up and I could walk. My legs were straight and strong and all in one piece. And all of a sudden, I wanted to walk for the Lord. I wanted to go wherever He told me, and find the people who needed help. Physical help, emotional help, spiritual help, I wanted to find them. I still do."

Tiffany saw Josh's eyes mist as the crowd clapped and whistled, and he met Tiffany's gaze, then handed her the microphone. She swallowed. "During the earthquake, I had a window shatter into my face and eyes. I don't know a word to describe the fear I felt. Everything went black, and then I fell through the floor and was buried like Mo and Josh. I couldn't move, and I thought I was going to die too. But Josh was a real hero. He made us reach for his hand, and we lay there and prayed. And God answered. We were found. The next morning, I was healed too. And I haven't seen the same since." She looked around the room. "I see more than faces now. I see people who are hurting, people who need help, people who need the Lord. But I can't get to them all, and neither can Josh or Mo. We did a lot together, but we need help. We need *your* gifts, all of them."

Mo took the microphone again. "This morning, the Lord led me to a passage in Romans 12."

Tiffany gasped as he opened his Bible and started to read. "'Just as each of us has one body with many members, and these members do not all have the same function, so in Christ we who are many form one body, and each member belongs to all the others.'"

Tiffany clutched her Bible against her chest. "Mo, He showed you that today? This morning?"

Josh touched both their arms and turned them around. "I read that too, first thing when I woke up."

The crowd grew quiet, watching, waiting, as Mo, Tiffany, and Josh stared at one another, their backs to the mike.

"He showed us that for a reason," Mo whispered. "All three of us. He wanted us to know what He was doing."

Josh started to laugh. "He was showing us that we have the gifts we need, as long as we all use them together."

Tiffany couldn't explain the joy rising inside her. "It's not punishment! The gifts were a temporary blessing, to show us the big picture."

Mo turned back to the microphone, and his voice rose with renewed confidence. "Sorry," he said. "As I was saying . . . we all have gifts. Every one of us who's in Christ. Supernatural gifts, powered by the Holy Spirit."

Tiffany spoke up. "There are lots of people out there hurting. Even before the earthquake, they were all around us. We just have to start looking . . . seeing . . . listening . . . going . . . telling . . ."

"Since the earthquake, it's gotten worse," Josh said. "People need us. They need the Lord. This church should be a spiritual triage unit, where the wounded and brokenhearted can come. This should be the place where people know they'll find Jesus."

The crowd erupted into whoops and cheers, and everyone sprang to their feet, applauding the task before them—and the One who had equipped them to fulfill it.

CHAPTER EIGHTEEN

*t*he sanctuary overflowed with seekers that morning—not just the fifteen Tiffany, Josh, and Mo had brought. Other members had extended invitations to friends and family, as well. Some visitors had gravitated to the church on their own, seeking to understand why such a devastating quake would rock their quiet little town.

The pastor and staff were ready. Thankfully, they had not insisted on following the bulletin's order of worship, but had made last-minute alterations to allow the Holy Spirit to work. And it was clear that He was in control.

The altar call at the end of the service drew people from all over the sanctuary, and Tiffany was startled to see not only strangers walking the aisle, but those who had attended their church for years. She understood why they came. Hadn't she sat in these pews week after week without ever taking her faith that seriously? The events of the past few days seemed to have awakened many of them. Sandy Miller and two of her friends walked to the front to join the others, followed by Dante and one of his "homeboys."

After the service was over, Tiffany hurried to the counseling room to congratulate Dante and Sandy and the others for their courage in announcing what they had done. Josh and Mo did the same, and the three of them stood outside the door, waiting for their friends to emerge.

Tiffany glanced at Josh's feet. "Still nothing?"

He shook his head. "I keep thinking it'll come back. Every now and then I feel like I need to go somewhere . . . like when I came here . . . but it's not as controlling as the gift was."

"Me too," Tiffany said. "I keep looking into people's eyes . . . waiting . . . and I do see things. I see pain and guilt and remorse. It doesn't take a whole lot to read people's faces. I could probably do that before . . . I just didn't. But it's not the same as those flash visions I was having. Who would have thought I'd be wishing for them when I was so freaked out at first?"

"I know," Mo said. "When I started talking, I felt like if I stopped, I'd dry up and blow away or something. Like the words were my life. But since the quake, I've spent a lot of time studying the Bible. Now I feel like I have a little more to stand on, you know? I know what the Bible says, and I can tell others. I have a long way to go, but I don't think I'll ever have that cool reserve I had before. There are too many people who need to hear."

When Mike approached them from the sanctuary, Tiffany could see that his eyes were red. He seemed fragile, as if he'd held back his feelings as long as he could, but wasn't sure how much longer he could manage it.

"I need a favor from you guys. A real big one."

"Sure," Tiffany said. "What is it, Mike?"

"See, my dad and I, we had a big fight. Remember I told you I sort of walked in on him with a girl who wasn't much older than me? I kept thinking of how he would break my mother's heart. I felt betrayed. Totally abandoned, like he'd chosen her over us . . . me."

"I don't blame you, man," Mo said.

"Only since I got to know Christ yesterday, I've been feeling like I need to go to him, you know? Forgive him. And tell him what you told me."

"Wow." Tiffany swallowed back the constriction in her throat. He was so young to the faith to have such an insight. "Wow."

"I was wondering if you guys would come with me. You know more than I do. I'll do most of it, since I have lots to say. But just in case he has a question that I can't answer, I thought it might help for you to be there."

Josh's mouth trembled as he patted Mike's back. "You got it, man. Wanna go right now?"

"Good a time as any," Mike said.

Dante came out of the room shortly after that, and reminded them about his grandmother. They told him they'd call him as soon as they were finished with Mike's dad.

Sandy had found a mentor. Jean Allen, who had recently

lost her son in a violent crime, had invited her to have lunch with her. From the depths of their suffering, the two had found a common bond.

As the trio started down the church's front steps with Mike, another church member stopped them. "I heard a guy was arrested last night, right after he accepted Christ," he said. "I do prison ministry on Sunday afternoons. I'd like his name if you've got it."

"Sure, man." Mo took the paper the man proffered, and wrote Ripper's name. "There were some others arrested, but I think they were bailed out. When do you think you'll see him?"

"We were thinking we would look him up today and try to disciple him while he's in jail."

Mo grinned at Tiffany and Josh. "Amazing. The body of Christ working together. I never thought I'd see the day."

CHAPTER NINETEEN

*m*ike drove the group to his home. The trepidation on his face was apparent as he got out of the car. "This isn't going to be easy. I haven't spoken to my father in weeks. And I've avoided my mom because I couldn't look her in the eye, knowing what I knew. I didn't want to tell her what Dad was doing. I couldn't stand the thought of breaking her heart like that."

Tiffany prayed silently as they followed him up the steps. Every muscle in her body felt as if it had petrified into stone. Her palms sweated and her heart raced. *Lord, help us to do some good here . . . even without our special gifts.*

Mike searched his key ring for the right key, then apparently thought better of just walking in. Slipping the keys back into his pocket, he rang the bell.

It took a few minutes, but finally his father answered the door. At the sight of his son, guilt and shame hooded his eyes. "Hello, Mike."

"Dad." Mike drew in a deep breath. "Is Mom here?"

He cleared his throat and scratched his forehead. "Uh . . . no. She's gone to visit your grandmother."

Mike swallowed and nodded. "Well, can we come in? I need to talk to you."

His father stepped back, allowing the four of them to enter. When he'd closed the door, Mike stood face to face with his father. "Dad, something happened to me yesterday, and my friends here were involved. I wanted you to meet them. Tiffany, Josh, and Mo, meet my dad, Greg Jefferson."

They each shook his hand, and Tiffany looked into his eyes. She saw the pain there, mixed among the guilt and shame, as well as fear of this confrontation with his son, and anxiety about what lay in his future.

He told them to sit down, so the three of them huddled next to one another on the couch. Mike's father took a chair that looked well worn, and Mike sat across from him.

"Dad, I've been in a real bad frame of mind since I walked in on you a few weeks ago."

Greg Jefferson shot a self-conscious look to the three on the couch.

"I told them," Mike said. "Yesterday, God sent these three to me. Led them right to the mall, into my store, and right up to my counter. I don't know how He did it. All I know is that He did. And we talked about forgiveness and restoration, and friendship with the God of the universe. And for the first time, I understood it."

His father stared at him for a moment, clearly confused. He must have expected lambasting accusations—not a testimony of God's grace. "Good, Mike. I'm glad for you."

Mike swallowed and struggled to keep the tears in his eyes from falling. "Dad, what I understood yesterday is that we all sin. Our sins hurt other people, ourselves, sometimes the ones we love the most. They also hurt God. And when I understood about the grace and forgiveness that I could have if I'd just submit to Christ, who died to take the punishment for my sins, I gave my life to Him."

Mike's father shielded his face with his big hand and started to cry. Tiffany wondered why. Was it relief that his son had come to Christ? Or was he acknowledging the magnificent grace of God?

The answer came the moment he looked up. "I wish I could have forgiveness like that."

Mike leaned forward. "Dad, you can."

He shook his head. "No. I've done some awful things. I followed my own impulses and broke my marriage vows. I crushed your mother and destroyed my relationship with you . . . and now I'm alone." He reached out to touch his son's shoulder. "Son, for what it's worth—and I realize it's not worth much—I've broken it off with the girl. It's over. I haven't seen her since that day. And I came clean with your mother. She didn't take it very well. But I really am so sorry."

Tiffany felt as if she didn't belong here. This was a private moment, and she and the guys were intruders. Still, she sat there quietly, praying for both men.

"I forgive you, Dad." Mike's soft voice held no trace of anger. "How can I not, when God forgave me? And the thing is, He can forgive you too. You can start over, clean."

His dad shook his head. "It won't save my marriage. It won't undo what I've done."

Mo planted his elbows on his knees. "Sir, you're right. It won't undo it, and it might be too late for your marriage. But with God, all things are possible. Jesus told us to seek first His kingdom and His righteousness, and all the things we need would be ours."

Mr. Jefferson got up and, rubbing the back of his neck, paced across the room. "That's just it. I can seek His righteousness until I'm blue in the face, but I can't *get* it. I've tried to do good. But the truth is that the woman Mike saw me with was not the first."

Tiffany glanced at Mike and saw the pain in his eyes. But there was still no anger.

"I've cheated on my wife for twenty-five years! When God looks at me, He must see a slimy coating of mud all over me. Why would He want to do anything for me?"

Tiffany spoke up. "Because it's *His* righteousness we're seeking," he said. "Not our own. The Bible tells us that our best, most righteous works are like filthy rags when compared to God's righteousness. There's no way we can ever make ourselves good enough to stand before God. So we have to rely on Christ to make us righteous."

"No way," Mr. Jefferson said. "He can't do it with me."

Josh got up and crossed the room, and stood face to face with the man who towered above him. "Why don't you give Him a chance and see? If Mike, a human being—your angry, hurt son—could forgive you, don't you think God could, too?"

. . .

A while later, the trio left the father and son alone. Mike's dad had not given his life to Christ just yet, but he wanted some private time with his son.

Josh had called Dante before they'd left and gotten his grandmother's address. He led them through town, to the neighborhood where the woman lived.

"Mr. Jefferson is so hung up on cleaning himself up first," Tiffany said. "He thinks he's got to change *before* he can come to God."

"Maybe it's more than that," Mo said. "Maybe he just wants to demonstrate his repentance first. That's important, you know. You can't really come to the cross without repentance. It doesn't work to keep those sins strapped on your back and try to walk with Christ. Repentance is key."

"Sounded like he'd repented," Josh said. "He sounded real remorseful."

"Repenting because you know your sins ruined your entire life is one thing," Mo said. "Repenting to God because you've sinned against Him is another."

Tiffany slowed her step as they entered a neighborhood that looked as though it should have been condemned and bulldozed years ago. "Maybe we just need to keep praying for him. God is obviously working in his life."

Josh rounded a corner, his step suddenly picking up speed.

"Josh, are you sure your feet aren't doing that thing again?" Tiffany tried to keep up. "This feels a lot like that."

"No, the address is leading me." Josh grinned at her. "I'm just anxious to get there."

Mo laughed. "Hey, did you see how we used our gifts back there? It wasn't exactly the same, but it didn't seem like we had entirely lost them, you know? Tiffany seemed to see right into the man; Josh, you had the same kind of courage you had with the feet thing; and I seemed to know just what to say."

Tiffany caught her breath. "Yes! And then it got even weirder, because we started overlapping. Josh and I spoke up. We knew what to say. I *never* know what to say."

"The last couple of days have built our faith," Josh said. "I don't think we're afraid anymore. We know that the Holy Spirit cares about these people, that He's there, helping us know where to go and what to see and what to say."

"That power just won't quit, will it?" Joy filled Tiffany as she spoke. "Even if we don't have supernatural feet and eyes and tongues." She slowed her step as they passed several dilapidated houses that were boarded up, noting the graffiti spray-painted on the walls. "Josh, where have you brought us?"

He stopped and looked down at the address in his hand. "Well, Dante warned us her house was in bad shape. That's why he wanted us to come."

Mo waved a hand in front of his nose. "Smells like the sewer is backed up. Man, how could anybody live in a place like this?"

Josh's eyes scanned the house numbers. "That house right there. That's where Dante's grandmother lives."

Mo gaped at the rotting house, with shingles peeling off the splintered roof, broken front steps, and duct tape holding the glass in the windows. "Man, somebody lives there? It looks terrible. Look at the front porch. You can't even get up to the door."

"We have to." Josh crossed the street to the house. Tiffany and Mo hung back as Josh stepped up carefully and took a giant step over the hole in the porch floor. He gave them a hand and helped them.

Josh knocked.

Dante opened the door. "Dudes! You made it."

He invited them into the dark house, and they looked past him to the decrepit old woman shuffling across the floor, coughing, leaning heavily on a cane. When she'd stopped coughing, Dante said, "Meet my grandma, Eliza Miller. Grandma, these are my friends."

Tiffany took the woman's bony hand, and started. It was hot! This woman was burning with fever.

"Here, sit down, ma'am." She tried to lead the wobbly woman to a chair, but Dante's grandmother resisted.

"I cain't sit down when I got company. Would you like some water?"

"No, thanks," Josh said. "We're fine."

Tiffany looked around. "We just want to visit with you. Do you mind if we turn on some lights?"

"Ain't got no lights," she said. "Couldn't pay the bill. They done turned 'em off."

"Come see this." Dante motioned for them to follow him up the hall. "You think the lights off is bad, you should see this." He took them into a dark room with nothing but a bed. Pointing to the mattress, he said, "Feel that."

Tiffany leaned over and felt the sheets. "They're soaking wet."

Dante nodded. "Roof's rotten. Last night's rain came through right on her bed. She had to sleep on the couch."

"It weren't so bad," the old woman said from the hallway. "Couch is right comfortable."

Tiffany thought of the old, humped-over woman trying to get comfortable on the dirty, torn sofa she'd seen in the living room. Old people were supposed to be protected, pampered. Not holed up in a place like this. "How could this happen? Doesn't she have anyone to help her?"

"She should." Dante slapped his own chest. "Except all her kin are just like me. We figured the government ought to be taking care of her, not us. While I was out there spending money on dope, my grandma didn't have no food. But I've changed now."

"You got that right," Mo said. He high-fived Dante.

"I'm taking care of my grandma from now on," Dante said.

"But I need some help, man. I don't have the money to buy her food and get her lights turned back on. She needs a doctor too. Her lungs sound terrible. She probably has pneumonia. And somebody's got to fix her roof. I'll do what I can, but I don't even know how to start, and I can't afford the stuff it'll take."

Tiffany sighed. "First things first. We need to get the lights and heat turned back on."

"That's not first," Josh said. "First we need to get her some food."

"No," Mo said. "First we need to get her some medical help."

Dante crossed his arms, sticking his hands under his armpits. "Well, I thought the first thing might be to pray."

Tiffany looked at Josh and Mo, and they all began to grin. "You're right, man," Mo said. "Thanks for reminding us. The first thing should always be to pray."

CHAPTER TWENTY

*J*osh ran home to get his mom's car, then brought it back, along with some tuna sandwiches his mother had made. The old woman devoured them.

"Now we need to call an ambulance," Tiffany said.

"No phone," Dante said.

Tiffany pulled her cell phone out of her purse. "I have this."

"I ain't going nowhere in no ambulance," the woman said. "I ain't dying."

"But you need to go to the hospital, ma'am."

"Take me in a car. My husband died in a ambulance, and I swore they'd never get me in one of them things." She started to cough.

Dante stroked her back until she'd calmed down. "He didn't die because of the ambulance. He was half dead when they got to him. But she gets these things in her head."

"We'll take her in my car," Josh said. "Just help me get her out there. I don't want her falling through the porch."

They carefully walked her out to the car, then took her to the emergency room. They waited while the ER staff did a chest x-ray and determined that she needed to be hospitalized.

Tiffany hoped they didn't stick her on a gurney in the hall. The woman was too ill to be put on hold. But when they came to admit her and took her straight to a room, she knew the Lord was answering their prayer.

Once in the room, Tiffany and the others helped Dante's grandmother get comfortable.

"At least she'll be warm here and have food and medicine." Tiffany fussed over the old woman's covers. "Mrs. Miller, we're going to leave you now, but while you're in the hospital we're going to take care of your house, okay?"

"How you gonna do that?" she asked. "You just kids. I'll be all right."

"We know people who can help," Mo said. "Our church is full of people who'll want to do for you."

They left Dante there and loaded back into Josh's car, and headed back to the church. It wasn't quite time for the evening service, and they found their pastor sitting in the sanctuary praying as he did before every sermon. They told him about the old woman.

Brother Jim's eyes seemed to come alive. "You've come to the right place," he said. "I've had calls all afternoon from people thinking about their effectiveness in God's kingdom. It's like a fire is burning under our members. They all want to put their gifts to use. I'll call a few of them back and tell them about Mrs. Miller, and tonight I'll mention her in my sermon. My guess is that we'll have her fixed up before she even gets home from the hospital."

A little while later, the church began to fill up. Sandy Miller was back, this time with about twenty of her sorority sisters, who filed into the pews, their faces shining with expectation.

Dante's friends from the gang came in, some of them still wearing their gang colors. But they didn't look as if they wanted to make trouble. They, too, walked in with an aura of reverence.

Other visitors filed in with long-time members, and Tiffany was overcome with gratitude that the Lord had chosen to work in so many people's lives. He had turned up the heat and activated His body so that every member would begin working for Him.

At the end of the service, the altar call drew another dozen people to the front. Tiffany watched as four of Sandy's friends went down to make their own professions of faith. Then two of Dante's friends went down, their faces serious with the decision they had just made.

Finally Tiffany saw Mike going down. She nudged Mo and Josh.

"I didn't know he was here," Mo whispered.

They watched with gentle smiles as he whispered to the preacher, wiping the tears on his face.

And then they saw a couple, walking slowly down the aisle.

"Mike's dad," Josh said.

Tiffany caught her breath. A small woman walked beside Mr. Jefferson, tucked beneath his arm. Pain and regret were evident in his twisted features, but he kept walking, drawing her with him.

"Mike's mother?" Mo whispered. "Do you think?"

Mike turned then and saw his parents coming, and his face collapsed in poignant relief. He started back up the aisle toward them, met them halfway, and took them both into his arms. They stood there like that for a long moment, clinging to each other and weeping, while the music of "Just as I Am" played on.

Tiffany sucked in a sob and dug through her purse for a tissue. Mo stuck his hand out. She looked up at him through her tears.

"I need one too," he said under his breath. She handed Mo one, then pulled another one out for Josh. He took it willingly and pressed it against his eyes as the family finished their walk down the aisle.

The trio left the church that night, and Tiffany felt the weariness that comes behind shed tears—and the intense satisfaction at seeing God's work.

"They're going to be all right," Mo said. "Mike's family is going to survive."

"Who would have thought?" Josh led them down the steps and back to his car.

Tiffany got into the front, and Mo sat in the back. "So do we go to the hospital now," Mo asked, "or to work on Dante's grandma's house?"

"The hospital," Tiffany said. "We need to talk to his grandmother about Christ. Then we can go back to the house. First things first."

They found the old woman sitting up in bed, enjoying her meal. Dante sat on the mattress next to her, helping her eat.

They visited until she'd finished, and when the tray had been taken away, she reached out for their hands. "You're good people."

Mo stepped up to the mattress and looked down into her face. "Thank you, ma'am, but we're really not. We're just God's people. He's the one who's good."

"Dante been telling me all about that." She patted her grandson's face. "How God changed his life. How Jesus saved him."

Tiffany smiled. "Really, Dante?"

He shrugged. "Hey, I wasn't gon' keep my own grandma in the dark, was I? She needs electricity, but she needs the Holy Spirit more."

The old woman pointed a bony finger at her chest. "Now, I got Him, too."

Just when she thought she had no more tears to shed, Tiffany began to cry as she hugged the old woman.

CHAPTER TWENTY-ONE

a line of cars sat parked in front of Mrs. Miller's dilapidated house when Tiffany and the guys made their way
back there. Mo had given Brother Jim the key, and he had
promised to bring help that night.

They went inside and found the lights shining brightly.
Brother Jim met them in the kitchen. "We had to get the
lights turned on so all this food could be refrigerated."

Tiffany looked around—at least a dozen casserole dishes
lined the freshly wiped counters. Another dozen grocery sacks
covered the table.

"Wow. Where did all this food come from?"

"Women in the church. All it took was telling a few people,
and the next thing I knew, everybody wanted to help."

"How did you get the lights turned on, on a Sunday?" Mo
asked.

Brother Jim grinned. "One of the executives at the light

company is a deacon in our church. He took care of it, and another member paid the bill."

Tiffany jumped as she heard pounding on the roof. "What's that?"

The pastor laughed. "Well, we're trying to get as much done as we can before dark. There's a carpenter in the choir who offered to bring what was needed over tonight and fix her roof. Tomorrow, he'll come back with the shingles. He and some other members plan to put a whole new roof on. Oh, and we have some more guys who are taking the day off work tomorrow to repair her porch and do some more work on the house."

Tiffany turned back to her two friends, her eyes shining with the reality of what had just happened. "The Body of Christ," she whispered.

Mo swallowed. "Every gift working together."

Josh took both of their hands in his. "And the Holy Spirit powering it all."

CHAPTER TWENTY-TWO

*J*osh drove Tiffany and Mo home that night. When he pulled in to her driveway, she made no move to get out.

"This was a good day," she whispered.

"Really good," Mo said.

"It's a little sad, though." Josh stared at the steering wheel. "I miss my gift."

"Me too," Tiffany said. "I felt so chosen there for a while. Like I had such an important purpose."

Mo leaned up on the seat. "You still have that purpose, Tiff. We all do. We were chosen, and we still have stuff to do."

"But it was cool having God move my feet like that."

"He can still move them, man."

Tiffany wiped the moisture under her eyes. "And it was really something, seeing what God sees."

"You still see it, Tiff. You saw it in Mike's dad. You saw it in Dante's grandma, even without the visions."

"You too, Mo," Josh said. "You still know what to say."

"Only because I've been studying my Bible," Mo said. "I can't stop. I'm gonna have to keep doing that, so I can be ready in season and out of season, just like the Good Book says."

"Me too," Tiffany said, and Josh nodded.

"I don't ever want to go back to the way I was before." Josh rubbed his steering wheel pensively. "Ignoring all those needy people around me, being as useless to the body of Christ as a paralyzed limb. I'm going to do my part from now on. I'm going to go where I'm told. Like Isaiah 52:7 says, 'How lovely on the mountains are the feet of him who brings good news, who announces peace and brings good news of happiness, who announces salvation, and says to Zion, "Your God reigns!"'"

Tiffany smiled. "I'm going to memorize that verse for myself too. He can use my feet. And from now on, I'm going to see with different eyes. What was that verse you gave me in the beginning, Mo?"

"Luke 10:23: 'Blessed are the eyes which see.'"

"Yeah. They *are* blessed, aren't they?"

"They sure are," Mo said. "And I'm never going to be quiet when God gives me the words. For now and the rest of my life, I'm going to speak the praises of God, like Zacharias did in Luke 1:64."

Tiffany breathed in a deep, shaky breath. "Well, good night, guys. It's been a real enlightening weekend." She opened the car door, but still didn't get out. Instead, she looked back at Josh, then at Mo. "We're still a team, aren't we? I mean, when school starts back up, we're not going to forget that we sort of—"

Josh grinned and shoved his glasses up. "Bonded?"

"Well, yeah," Tiffany said. "We weren't exactly the best of friends before. We were practically at each other's throats that day in the darkroom."

Mo groaned. "Yeah, the things that seem so important . . . Seems like a long time ago, doesn't it?"

"A whole lifetime," Tiffany whispered.

Josh looked over at her. "I'm not gonna forget you guys. But I'm still the nerd. You guys might want to forget about me."

"You're not a nerd," Tiffany said. "You're a hero. My brother."

Josh looked at her as if her words surprised him. She reached across the seat and took his hand, just as she'd done under the rubble. Josh reached back and took Mo's hand, and Mo closed the circle.

They sat like that, holding hands and remembering the fear, the miracles, the mighty works.

"We're still part of God's dream team," Mo whispered. "The body of Christ."

Suddenly hand holding was not enough. Tiffany reached over and hugged Josh, then turned to the backseat and embraced Mo. Finally she got out of the car.

As she walked up to her front door, Mo got into the front seat, and Josh sat, letting the vehicle idle as he waited for her to go in. She stopped inside the doorway and waved, and they started to back out of the driveway.

"All for One, and One for all," she whispered.

It had always been the plan.

More from TERRI BLACKSTOCK

The Gifted

Three ordinary Christians are given three extraordinary gifts of the Holy Spirit, making them a spiritual dream team.

The Heart Reader

For two weeks, Sam Bennett is given an extraordinary gift: hearing as God hears. Frightened at first, he begins to use his gifts to touch others and radically transform his own life.

The Heart Reader of Franklin High

What if you could hear as God hears? Jake Sheffield can. He can hear the deepest needs of people around him, although they aren't saying anything. Is Jake going crazy, or is God about to do something amazing?

Covenant Child

Twins Kara and Lizzie grew up in squalor, never guessing the riches held in trust for them or the love that lived to call them home. Now they must choose between the familiar and the extraordinary.

PUBLISHING GROUP™
www.wpublishinggroup.com